Strange And Twisted Things

Copyright © 2023 by Holly Payne-Strange

Holly Payne-Strange asserts the Moral Right to be identified as the Author of this work.

No part of this publication may be reproduced, distributed, or transmitted in any form or by any means, including photocopying, recording, or other electronic or mechanical methods, without the prior written permission of the publisher, except as permitted by U.S. copyright law.

ISBN: 9798853570924

Book Cover by Nejc Planinšek

Line Editing by Sarah De Souza

Printed In the United States of America

All rights reserved.

To those eight wild days,
The woman who survived them
And the man who inspired them
και στην Αφροδίτη, προστάτιδα αυτού του βιβλίου

CONTENTS

1. Chapter 1 — 1
2. Chapter 2 — 16
3. Chapter 3 — 27
4. Chapter 4 — 39
5. Chapter 5 — 49
6. Chapter 6 — 66
7. Chapter 7 — 75
8. Chapter 8 — 86
9. Chapter 9 — 98
10. Chapter 10 — 109
11. Chapter 11 — 117
12. Chapter 12 — 129
13. Chapter 13 — 144
14. Chapter 14 — 150
15. Chapter 15 — 160
16. Chapter 16 — 187
17. Chapter 17 — 194

18. Chapter 18	205
Epilogue	214
Acknowledgements	219
Also By	221

Chapter One

She was surprised how much it hurt. It's not that she thought it would be easy – simply that she had never considered it at all. At seventy-two, Greta had assumed she would become a widow, not a divorcee. So when her usually attentive and thoughtful husband served her papers, she didn't even respond. She had no idea what to say.

She had never doubted that she loved him more than he loved her – it had been obvious in so many ways. She was always the one to make peace after a fight, the one to remember dates, details, facts. Everything from his preferred dishes at restaurants to his mother's birthday, she knew. More than that, she would do anything, anything for him at all. But she had been happy. Who wouldn't be, with a man like him? Sweet, handsome, funny, kind. Smart as a whip. Even now she had nothing bad to say about him – well, apart from the fact that he had ruined her life.

Still, he took care of her. Made sure that the divorce settlement had been fair, fair enough for her to buy a new house outright. Not a perfect one, there were certainly problems with it – the pipes were rusting, the electrics were spotty at best, there was a hole in one of the walls. After all, it had been abandoned for 50 years. And even then, it had only been owned briefly.

But she had fallen in love with it. It was old, like her. Unwanted, like her. It was by the sea – not quite on the beach, but close enough that at night she could hear the waves crash. The windows were tall, letting in huge bands of sunlight, and she could already imagine the way they would illuminate her Moroccan rugs, her velvet couch. The spiral staircase that reached all the way to the third floor was carved from delicate mahogany. And almost every wall was heavily decorated with Victorian frescos depicting ancient Roman myths. She adored them.

Of course, having a clearly English building in the middle of Tuscany was strange, to say the least. It looked as if an old British manor house had been picked up and plonked down on the Italian coast. Odd. But that was another way in which it was like her – a wild mix of places and cultures, bound to nothing, indebted to nothing.

The home was beautiful, she had decided, with only a few minor flaws. And those, she was determined to fix. That was one of the most valuable skills her mother had taught her – put your pain into things. Don't just sit with it. Let it move you, let it create something beautiful.

Her shoulders still hurt, both from the constant tension of crying and the fact that at her age, bodies simply hurt sometimes. But at least the pain had meaning now. She put it to work for her, using it as fuel to create. And she would create something beautiful.

But now, finally – it was hers. The movers had been late, of course, and it had taken the entire day to move her things up from Naples, what should have been a five-hour drive somehow stretching into almost double that. How, she had no idea, although she suspected it had something to do with them being paid by the hour.

It was too late to start unpacking now, the crisp autumn night closing tightly around her, the lemon trees casting a long shadow through the massive windows. She was prepared, of course. That morning she had booked a room at the local hotel, knowing full well how late everything would go. Well, it was local enough. This was a small village, with nowhere to stay and no real reason for outsiders to do so. Still, she was thrilled to be there. It was so different to Naples, that bustling, vibrant, but undeniably grimy city. This was quaint, almost cute. The Etruscan coast was so close you could practically taste it, the air brighter and fresher somehow. And the little houses that dotted the village reflected that, a well kept joy in their bright colors and sweet little window boxes. Against them, her house certainly stood out.

Finally, finally the movers had left, the papers were signed and the house was hers. All hers. It was thrilling, in a way. She certainly hadn't thought to start again this late in life, but it wasn't all bad, she reflected, as she took her first steps inside. So many ideas sprang to mind, so many exciting projects to be done. The stairs would need carpets, (they would have to be custom, because of its unusual shape, and appropriately regal, of course) paintings would have to be hung too, and of course there were the Christmas decorations. For the first time in a long time, she smiled.

The electrics were old, and there was barely a working bulb in the whole house. Still the moon shone in, gifting everything with a gentle silver glow. There was only one word for it; enchanting.

But it was cold. So cold, colder in one room than in the others, which was strange. To test the theory she wandered into the kitchen, peering around in the gloom. Yes, it was certainly warmer in there. And then, back into the living room. Ice cold, again. She drew her shawl around her, suddenly uneasy, though she was determined not to fall prey to superstition and fear. It was probably a draft, and she chided herself for thinking anything else.

She hadn't been into the basement yet. Even when she was looking around with the realtor, she had done no more than poke her head inside the door. The long, grimy stairs had seemed slightly ominous even then, and she hadn't wanted to take her chances with the clearly unstable banister. Besides, she had already fallen in love with the place. She didn't need to go down and ruin it for herself.

She was just admiring the hallway, with its depiction of Venus and mercury, when she heard it.

Thud, thud, thud.

Her blood ran cold. It sounded almost like footsteps, but much, much heavier. And besides, she was alone, completely alone in the house. Suddenly she thought of just how long this place had stood empty, who else might have keys, or what animals might have decided to claim it.

At her age, and with her fake hip, running wasn't a viable option. But she tried. With the *Thud, thud, thud* seeming to be right behind her, she shuffled forward, her own body betraying her, forcing her to linger and witness the newly hostile house – the shadows that lurked in every room, the cobwebs that now seemed monstrous and looming, the too-real faces that scowled down at her from the frescoes. She had no choice but to take it all in as she meandered towards the door, begging her legs to go just a little faster.

Heart hammering, moving as quickly as she could, she shuffled out the front door not daring to stop and see if she was being followed. It wasn't easy, even for a young and fit person, it would have been hazardous. The house was located at the top of a large hill, and as she hurried out, she stumbled, the thin set of stairs uneven beneath her feet. Her heart leapt into her throat, certain for one mad moment that something was going to come and get her.

It wasn't until she was safely in the car that she realized how ridiculous she was being. She let out a frightened little chuckle. Of course there were strange things in that house. It *was* a strange house! She'd never been inside alone before, let alone at night, it was only natural there would be some surprises. Besides, if there was anyone in the house, the movers would have noticed! And they all left ages ago, she said goodbye to them each. She knew it couldn't be them, knew it couldn't be anything sinister in fact. *Old fool,* she thought to herself, squaring her shoulders and taking a deep breath. She drove down the coast slowly, cautiously, fully aware that really, she should not be driving at night. Her eyesight wasn't really up to it. But it was quiet, almost deserted in fact, and the crashing waves were so peaceful, so calming, it seemed impossible to be afraid.

No, she wouldn't let herself be silly now. There was nothing wrong with the house, apart from the fact that Frederick wasn't there, and there was nothing to be done about that. In fact, it was marvelous, and when she was done with it, it would be even better, she was sure of it. Situated on a remote part of the Italian coastline, far away from any disturbances, it was the perfect place for a quiet soul such as herself.

But still, it was strange, having absolutely no one to talk to. She didn't like it. She felt a cold chill crawl up her spine as she wondered just how long it would go before she said a word. A week? A month? More? Would her voice become hoarse and croaky with disuse, her words harder and harder to find?

Of course, she told herself, she was being ridiculous. Her brother would call, as he always did, asking for money. They would probably even fight, both battling it out in a shouting match that would make her throat sting. And she knew she could call Mary-Beth any time. But that woman's health was so poor, Greta didn't like to be a burden. And besides, it always came back to her latest hospital visit anyway.

She cared, of course she did, the woman was her best friend. But still, it did get old after a time.

They had met at school and been fast friends ever since, two foreign kids finding a natural affinity with each other. Greta was from Germany, Mary-Beth from America, neither knew the slightest bit of Italian, finding that they simply had to fail their way through, eventually getting the hang of it through trial and embarrassing error. She found she was proud of it now, proud of how well she had acclimatized. She thought of herself as being utterly Italian – after all, she had lived in Italy for most of her life. Her father was a restorer of medieval paintings, and her parents had moved there for work when she was only nine. She embraced it as her home now, loving everything about the country, from the hustle and bustle of Rome to the towering Dolomites, unable to see herself living anywhere else. Certainly unable to see herself moving far from Mary-Beth, who had been in her life for over six decades. She knew she would always be able to rely on her

No, she found, that wasn't quite what she meant. She knew she had people she could call in an emergency. But she wanted someone to *talk* to. To chat with. About the small and mundane parts of her day. About how she would probably need a new kettle soon, although she reckoned she could get a few more weeks out of this one. Or about how the local new station constantly mispronounced the word caramel (why were they talking about it that much anyway?). Or that she was sure they had changed the recipe for her favorite sliced bread, it just tasted *different* up here. Not better or worse, but different. Things like that. Stupid things.

People say that these twitterings have no substance. "Small talk", they call it, as if it was so minor and useless compared to the Big Conversations about art or literature or whatever high brow things people thought were somehow better. As if they talked about those things anyway, they didn't. Not really, not often.

Finally, she arrived at her hotel. It was thoroughly Tuscan, an old stone villa made warm with glowing floodlights, its white windows decked with deep purple curtains and a roaring fire just visible from inside. *God Fredrick would love this*, she suddenly realized. It took everything in her not to get out her phone and text him. That was one of the problems with modern technology; he was never more than one bad decision away. She tried not to focus on that, instead taking in her surroundings. They were at the very top of a hill, and around them, just visible in the soft moonlight, were countless vineyards. Little squares of cultivated earth, emphasized by pricks of yellow light, spilling out from the farmhouses, while roads dotted with cypress trees snaked their way through the valleys. It was utterly charming and serene, even at night. This was the peace she had been looking for.

The next morning she woke bright and early, a knot in her stomach. She couldn't tell if it was anticipation or fear. She felt faintly embarrassed now, about how she had run away last night, although there had been no one there to judge. She contemplated the issue as she pulled her skirt on, a nice, rose pink thing made of chiffon and lace. On the one hand, she didn't think she was completely insane. She hadn't imagined it. But on the other, she was tired, and she was under a huge amount of stress. That simply did things to the mind, made a person on edge, jumpy, prone to misunderstandings. She was sure there was some kind of reasonable explanation for everything, and she was determined to find it.

She drove back cautiously, still not used to the winding country roads. But still, she couldn't help but be excited. Approaching the house filled her with such joy, she thought she would sing. It was magnificent, even in its currently reduced state. With its duck egg blue balcony and dark, almost gothic black shingle roof, it simply exuded history and beauty. Just behind it, the maze was visible, a colossal mystery of verdant green, wildflowers spewing from its entrance.

She took the hill cautiously this time, holding onto the railings perhaps a little more tightly than necessary. The concrete steps were a bit cracked, she could see that now. Nothing a little elbow grease wouldn't fix, but still. She hadn't noticed before.

That day, she decided to begin in her new kitchen. It was tiny, certainly not big enough for two people. Light blue cupboards lined the walls, the gray countertops heaving with her boxes. She'd have to deal with those soon. She picked one at random. It didn't have relevant supplies in it, which royally annoyed her. It seemed to simply be a box of junk, with the occasional spoon thrown in, so that the professional movers could label it 'kitchen' and call it a day. And then something caught her eye.

She cleared her throat, heart hammering. She was about to do something stupid, and a bit reckless. At least for her.

"Hello dear," she said, lifting out a stuffed toy owl Fredrick had got her the last time they had been on holiday together. "We got you in Florida, you know." She felt incredibly foolish, resisting the urge to look around and see if anyone was laughing at her, though she knew she was perfectly alone.

"Long way you've come." She tried again, looking down at its plush white belly. She hadn't touched it much, while he'd been around. A little, of course. It had made her smile when her eyes had grazed upon it, she had given it the odd pat on the head once in a while. But she had never really been one for stuffed toys, and so she let it linger on the shelf. Never did she think it would be her only companion.

"We were truly happy then. At least, I was. Having him near me was...electric. Even after all those years. We were married 48 years, you know." She stroked its front again, touched its rough beak. "I just don't understand. It's not like he left me for another woman. I didn't do anything wrong." And here her voice broke. "I didn't gamble our money away or call him names. I wasn't an old shrew that nagged him constantly. I only ever wanted to make him happy. And he'd rather be alone." She had to stop, a sudden wave of nausea overwhelming her. It hurt so much. She squeezed the owl into her stomach, which actually did help, a little at least. It seemed to artificially fill an ache she had, a hole inside her. She knew it was stupid. Still, it was nice to get a little hug.

"I think I shall get a cat," she proclaimed, setting the owl down gently on the kitchen counter. Floppy, she decided, looking at it. Its name would be Floppy. Both because that's how it acted, not really able to stay standing upright, slowly sliding down the box she had propped it up against. And because that's how she felt, needing him. Floppy. As if she had only a general idea of herself, of what to do, what to think, how to act. It was all a bit...vague. Listless. She knew the slightest suggestion could move her in any direction, as she had none of her own.

It was then the doorbell rang.

She jumped about a mile, rushing to the door, hoping she hadn't been heard. On her porch stood a young man, surely not out of his twenties yet, long hair in his eyes, a bright smile on his face, and a pie in his hands.

"Hi," he said, as she slowly pushed the heavy door open, followed by some slew of gibberish she couldn't understand.

She looked at him, puzzled. God, how she hated this, hated how she had to explain to every person she met that they had to speak up. How they inevitably just ended up yelling at her.

"What do you say, dear?" she asked, a knot of worry in her stomach. What would he think of her?

But he just smiled, stretched out his hand, and said – in a much louder voice this time – "I'm Davide, from just down the road. Thought I'd welcome you to the neighborhood."

Neighbors. She could talk to neighbors. How had she forgotten that? She certainly was floppy.

"Davide," she said, smiling back. "How nice to meet you. I'm Greta. I would invite you in, but I hardly have anything unpacked yet. I could do tea?" Suddenly she wished she had already replaced that kettle.

"Oh, you are so kind. But I am afraid I can not. I am on my lunch break. It's just so nice to see this place occupied again. I've lived here most of my life, you know, never seen anyone even attempt to take it on."

She drew herself up proudly. "Well, a little hard work never frightened me. Besides, it's going to be so beautiful when it's back to its former glory. Built in the 1840s, you know!"

"Of course!" he said, his smile growing bigger. "I'd love to talk to your son about it– "

"My son? I don't have any children." She said, her brow creased in confusion.

"Or, well, you know. Whoever is doing most of the work." He said, shifting his feet nervously.

"That would be me," she said simply, knowing exactly what was coming.

His face froze. "Oh. Oh my goodness, I am so sorry, I guess I just thought– You know, it's a lot of work–"

She decided to put him out of his misery. "I know I may look like an ancient, dried out husk–"

"No no no no–" He said quickly, his face turning pale.

"But I am in fact quite handy. The first home I bought wasn't unlike this. Maybe even worse. This place is in remarkably fine condition, all things considered." She stood a little taller, proud to know these things. She had done her research.

"But it's barely been updated since the 1800s! The previous owners did not even have time to update the plumbing. You know that right?" He asked, as if she had gone mad.

"Of course I know, it's my house." She huffed, unused to being questioned in such a fashion. He must have realized because he began to splutter.

"I, of course. It's just, you know. One person. I couldn't imagine doing it all myself. I'm not handy you see! Maybe I'll have to call you next time, ha!" He said, rambling on and on, clearly mortified.

It reminded her of Frederick. She let out a long, low sigh, determined not to burst into tears in front of this nice young man. Instead, the thought actually made her smile. She wondered what on earth he'd do. Die of shame, probably. Making the little old lady cry, he'd never forgive himself. Part of her wanted to do it, thought it might be funny.

But she resisted this impish urge. Instead, she just smiled and patted him on the arm. "Call me any time. You know where to find me."

"Thanks. Alright, well, I have to dash. Lunch break and everything. But I really am interested in talking about the house. Such history! When I was a kid, we used to– Well. You don't want to hear about that, and I really do have to go– I'm on my lunch break! I said that already, didn't I? Sorry. Anyway, let's catch up sometime. Nice to meet you." And with that, he practically sprinted off, jogging back in even deeper humiliation to actually hand over the pie.

"Sorry. Must be out of my mind today! It's peach. My husband made it. He's American," he said, as if that explained anything. "Anyway. Uh, bye." And this time he really did leave.

She couldn't help but smile after him. It wasn't his fault he had underestimated her. Had made assumptions. Almost everyone did.

She hadn't been exaggerating, she really did think she could handle most of the house alone. Frankly, the main issue was that it was filthy. Years of dust and filth, of neglect and hardship had all accumulated to make a truly overwhelming mess. That was certainly what she was going to have to deal with first, even before she unpacked most of her things. She hoped that Floppy wouldn't get too dirty, making a mental note to clear a spot for him soon.

She set to work. Putting her headphones on and selecting a good podcast, she happily whiled away the day. She started in her bedroom, of course. It was nice to have the pressure, to know that if she didn't get the filth out of the room, the mattress down, the sheets on and the pillows fluffed, she simply wouldn't have anywhere to sleep that night. It focused her mind, which was a blessing. Every moment she wasn't thinking about Fredrick was a gift.

Outside of these distractions, her torment was acute, and the ache with which she missed him simply would not cease. She would sometimes scream inside her head – not out loud, that would be too much, too attention grabbing, and she didn't need that. It was simply a primal...something welling up inside her that could not be expressed by words. Inside her head she would scream, and scream, and scream. Howling might be the right word. She found it helped. Either way, it could not be avoided.

For now, she was grateful to focus on the task before her.

The entire room was filthy. It had to be scrubbed from top to bottom, walls and all. She would have done the ceiling if she could reach it. But the rest, she did. Did it so well, in fact, that she had time to mop the kitchen floors too, remarking to Floppy as she did about how hideous they were, covered in garish linoleum. One of the very few renovations from the 1960s the previous owners had been able to complete.

It was with great satisfaction that, finally, Greta fell into her freshly made bed. The room was hardly decorated at all, not yet. But what was there was glorious, a massive bronze lamp with red beads, a very art deco style. An old chest of drawers that brought to mind some far away place, with its carved dragons and ornate drawer pulls. And then of course there was her side table, a gift from her dear grandmother. She already had a neat stack of books on it, little compact promises of adventures yet to come. For now though, she climbed into bed and gathered the soft yellow comforter around her, as if to keep the memories at bay. It almost worked. At least she was so physically exhausted that she was able to fall asleep easily and quickly, something she hadn't been able to do for a long time.

If only it could have stayed that way.

It was about four a.m. when she next awoke, the house around her creaking and sighing. She rolled over, a hand reaching out instinctively for Fredrick. She wondered briefly when that would stop happening.

But then.

A tap was running. Somewhere downstairs, it must be the kitchen. Her heart froze, the hair on the back of her neck standing up. Those were old faucets, heavy and rusted. They wouldn't have moved easily. They hadn't for her, when she had made her nighttime tea. She'd had to brace her other hand against the wall, turning it with an almighty tug that left her hand red and sore. Someone must have been down there.

Selfishly, she wished Fredrick was here. Again. He never would have made her go down alone.

She dearly wished she could simply bury her head under the covers, wait for it all to go away. But she couldn't. Boxes and boxes of her things were still down there, most of her art, her clothes. Her wedding photos, she realized with a twinge in her chest.

She couldn't let go of those.

Heart hammering and hands shaking, she threw back the covers. Gathering her dressing gown around her and having the foresight to slip her cell phone into her pocket, she tiptoed to the staircase, looking down. The smell was awful. Putrid and decaying, halfway between manure and rotten fruit.

Legs trembling, she gripped the banister with both hands. Step by step, she drew closer to the sound.

As she had suspected, it was coming from the kitchen, the sink overflowing with brown water which splashed onto the floor. With deepening terror, she whipped around. No one was there. More to the point, she didn't see how anyone *could* be there. The front doors were so heavy and screeching, there was no way that anyone would have been able to sneak in. The windows had been painted shut, and none of them were broken. The back door was firmly locked.

"Hello?" she called out, though the last thing she wanted was a response. For one terrible, heart stopping moment, she felt sure she was about to see an apparition, some specter of death to carry her away. But she couldn't just stop.

She crept forward, feeling like a fugitive in her own home, shuffling towards the tap. Thankfully, it turned off easily, the sudden silence shocking. She reached her hand into the deep basin, wondering what on earth could have clogged it. She touched something soft and slimy. With a deep breath for courage and gritted teeth, she pulled it out.

"Floppy." She breathed, looking at the now rancid owl. She couldn't help but cry.

Chapter Two

She was much calmer the next morning. Though she certainly had a lot on her mind, she felt like she could actually deal with it now. Sleep always centered her, gave her a fresh perspective on things. And besides, it was hard to be afraid with bird song in the air and a fresh pair of socks on. Floppy must have simply fallen into the sink, she decided as she sipped her tea, sitting, for the first time, on her very own balcony, looking out over the lemon trees and pink autumn crocuses. Wasn't he slipping down when she saw him last? These things can move very slowly, sometimes. Like her, she thought with a rueful smile. It must have just taken a very, very long time for him to fall. That wasn't so unusual, was it?

The fact was, something strange *had* happened in the house, but she had immediately flown to the wildest and most dramatic conclusion. Ghosts and the grim reaper! Madness. She had been fiddling with the taps yesterday. When she made her tea. That was probably the first time that they had been used since god knows when. Was it really that surprising that there had been some kind of reaction? No, it wasn't. She was just tired, lonely, and stressed. She had overreacted. She felt a little silly now, crying over a soft toy.

She had scrubbed him clean, spritzed him with rose water and was now letting him dry out in the sun.

What concerned her, far more than anything supernaturally sinister, was the realistic possibility that she might actually be going mad from grief. She had once thought that was entirely the purview of Shakespearean heroines, or leads in overly dramatic soap operas. But now...with how worked up she was getting about everything... it didn't seem entirely impossible.

She flinched a little. She didn't want that for herself, didn't want to just waste away. It seemed so sad, so pointless. But it just couldn't be anything else, there was no other explanation.

"No, Floppy." She said, patting the little owl on the top of the head. "What's more likely, that a little old woman is losing it a bit, or that this place is somehow haunted? I've got to sort myself out. Get control. Put my thoughts in order. I don't want to let go of Frederick, but...perhaps I have...over indulged a little. I need to put this out of my mind, throw myself into the house. Focus on something else." She grit her teeth. Why, oh why was she being asked to give up even the memory of him. God it was awful. Was there nothing left for her? That seemed brutally and cripplingly unfair. A spark of anger raged inside her, just for a moment.

"But on the other hand..." She breathed, stroking his fat fluffy belly. "There's no use fighting fate. I would be happier, in a house haunted by him, than all alone."

And it was true. She firmly believed she was going mad, making connections that didn't exist, experiencing things that weren't there. But she was entirely unwilling to sacrifice her love to fix that issue.

"I'll call a plumber," she promised. "Get this old house in order a little more. Then we will see."

She looked down at Floppy and let out a long sigh. He was still just a little brown.

She vowed to find a better place for him. She briefly wondered if it would be silly to sleep with him in her bed, and then decided, well, screw it. It was her house, and she was, of course, utterly and completely alone. She blushed, realizing that maybe she had imagined the dripping taps because she *hoped* someone was there. That maybe having anyone, even an intruder, was preferable to living alone. Her mother had always said she "loved too hard". Well, perhaps. But it seemed rather too late to do anything about that now. She turned her attention back to the house instead

It was the floors that really bothered her, dusty and mysteriously sticky under her feet. And this was a massive house. Even if she was able to clear one room a day, as she had with her bedroom, it would still take her almost a month to fully finish.

Perhaps she should call her brother. He would help her; they were siblings after all. She'd helped him the last time he had got into a pickle. It had cost her almost four thousand euros, but she had done it. It was with an air of slight entitlement that she picked up the phone and called him.

He came, as she knew he would, he was her elder brother after all, obligated to help his sister. But he did grumble about it. She knew he would do that, too. And so she forced herself to smile as he drove up her long driveway, promising herself she would stay civil- no matter how much he moaned.

"Wow," Mark said, getting out of his car and gazing up at it. "This is massive. How big is it?" Greta winced at what he was wearing, paint splattered jeans and an old T-shirt. She told herself not to judge, they were cleaning all day, after all. But still, it looked faintly ridiculous on a man of his age, especially as his features were so delicate, even boy-ish.

"Three stories. Four if you count the basement," she told him proudly. "I'll have to show you the garden at one point. There's a maze! It's overgrown, but still. Must have been beautiful once. Will be beautiful again, one day." She was already mentally ordering flowers. It needed more herbs she decided, something to cook with, a fragrance to waft through the air at night. Currently, it was all a bit of a mess. To the side of the house was a laburnum tree, the last yellow flowers clinging to its thin frame, while in front was a flock of flower beds. Clearly, they had been perfectly manicured, once upon a time. Now they were largely sickly looking ferns and patchy hellebore. She didn't really understand why the maze at the back thrived so much, although she supposed it must get significantly more sunlight.

"I can see why you wanted some help," he said, making his way up the staircase that led to the front door.

She led her brother inside, imploring him to ignore the boxes that were stacked precariously in every room, and down into the basement. It seemed fitting to start at the lowest point and work their way up. The basement was the filthiest room in the house, and she wasn't sure how long her brother was planning on sticking around for. If she could only get help with one area, this was the one to pick.

She handed him a spray bottle and a roll of paper towels, gesturing for him to get dusting. He looked at her as if she had just handed him a python and told him to get snake charming.

"God. Frederick couldn't even buy you a clean home, eh? I'm sorry he turned out to be such a bastard." Mark said, lips pursed. Greta's heart jumped. Hearing his name was still painful.

"Don't say that. He was an extremely good husband," she declared, soft but sure. "The best man I ever knew. And I picked this house." She started to pick up litter from the ground, getting everything out of the way so she could sweep.

"You're talking about him as if he were dead," Mark said, raising an eyebrow.

"I'm not," she said, putting a crisp packet into the rubbish bag she was holding. "I'm just not angry at him."

"It'll come," he said with an air of fake wisdom.

"I hope not," she countered. "He deserves to be happy."

At this, he raised an eyebrow. He had been there in the days after she received the news. She had stayed with him a little while. She had not been able to stop crying, hadn't even been able to get out of bed some days. He couldn't fathom that level of loyalty.

"Some people really are that good, you know. So good that they can hurt you. Deeply, profoundly. And you love them anyway. I know I sound like a mad old bag. But..." And here she stopped, blinking back tears and looking up at the ceiling.

"But I really do love him that much. I'm not hiding anything. I'm not putting a brave face on it. I am deeply and horrifically sad. Constantly. But I'm not angry. He did what he thought was best. And how can you be angry at someone for doing that?"

"I could have killed Maria, when she left me," he muttered.

"Maria and you had a very tempestuous relationship. Not worse," she added, before he could butt in. "But it was always fiery. My Frederick...he was so kind. So genuinely kind. Always doing things for others. Always, I used to worry he'd kill himself, bending over backwards for people. And so smart. He always had something clever and witty to say, no matter what the subject was, I remember..."

"Oh, God! Will you please stop?" her brother yelled, his face screwed up in a scowl. She had always hated that expression on him, it ruined his soft features, making a mockery of them somehow. As if it were unnatural, that someone with such a delicate face could be so cruel. "I can't clean *and* listen to you jabber on like a lovesick fool all day! I mean...this is insanity! Don't you want to start getting over him?"

"No," she said with a finality that shocked even her. "I'm not ready to let go of a love like that. I don't have any hope of a reconciliation, of course. I'm not that foolish. But...I'm not letting go of the love I felt. It was wonderful And...and to be honest, I don't think I'm going to find it again. So, no. I don't want to let go of it."

"You know you're coming across as rather desperate. He didn't want you." He pointed out, dusting down a shelf.

She physically flinched at his words. "I know. I failed to impress. But the feeling is not mutual. Do I regret it? Yes. Will it stop me? No."

He didn't have any idea what to say to that, and so they worked for a while in silence, clearing two rooms between them. She was glad he didn't push her, because she didn't feel that she could fully explain herself. Other than, well, love was beautiful.

It felt good, to love.

Hate was ugly, anger was exhausting, sadness was a pit she feared she would never, ever crawl out of. But love... reciprocated or not... that was sublime. Sacred. In fact, she fancied, love that was not returned was perhaps even more impressive, considering the pain involved in maintaining it.

There was nothing pathetic about it. It was stubborn and wild and unrelenting. But she kept it to herself, luxuriating in the silence. In the secret.

Until..."What's this?" he asked, pulling at a doorknob.

"It's a door, Mark. I'm surprised you haven't seen one before," she replied lightly. He rolled his eyes.

"Yes, but where does it go? It won't open." He rattled it again. "Besides, it's...kind of creepy."

To be fair to him, it was. It was bright red, with concentric circles burned into the wood, a stark difference to the easy elegance of the rest of the house.

"I'm sure I have the key somewhere," she said dismissively. "The realtor gave me a few of them when I signed the papers."

"That's a relief. Creepy old house that creaks in the night, door that won't open in the basement. I was starting to think this was a haunted house." He nudged her playfully in the ribs.

But her mouth went dry, the events of last night still playing on her mind. It was just a joke, she told herself. And he wasn't to know why it was in bad taste. She forced a smile.

"How do you know this place creaks in the night? You haven't stayed here yet." She pointed out.

"No, but look at it. It's bound to, old thing like this."

She felt tension she didn't know she was carrying leave her shoulders. Of course it would. She had always known that, but it was so nice to have it confirmed by an outside source. She silently chided herself for being a fool.

And so it was with a much warmer heart that she invited him to dinner. "Can't do much more than aglio e olio, I'm afraid. Only found one pan so far."

With a smile, they sat down, using boxes as both chairs and tables, setting their plates of spaghetti and mugs of wine down wherever they found space. It certainly wasn't how Greta envisioned using her dining room, but, well. It was a start.

"So, we haven't discussed a rate for today yet," Mark said as he tucked into his dinner.

"What?" She replied with a half laugh, certain he was joking.

"You know, my day's rate. Payment," he said through a mouthful of food.

"I – I thought you were here as my brother?" she said, a horrible sinking feeling in her stomach.

"What?" He asked, looking at her as if she had just said something disgusting. "I'm a painter and decorator Greta. This is what we do. This is our job."

"What – no. You were a painter for what, six months, thirty years ago? And you got fired? I hardly think that counts. I barely even remembered you were one." In truth, she didn't mean to sound so rude. She was quite simply, stunned. And those were the facts.

"Oh, so now you're insulting me," he said, throwing his fork down. "I should have known you were too tight fisted to even – "

"Siblings are supposed to be there for each other. Especially in times of need like this." She said, slowly, admitting it to herself as well as explaining it to him.

"I let you stay with me when your husband kicked you out!" he said indignantly.

"You charged me rent then as well." It came out before she could stop herself.

"It's just what's fair," he said. "A person works, they get paid, that's how it is. Are you trying to rip off your own brother?" He spat the words out, as if she was the unreasonable one.

"No." She had no idea how things had turned like this, how she was suddenly the bad person. She was sure she had made it clear that this was a favor, that this was simply what you did for the family. She would have done it for him. Had done far more in the past.

"Good!" he said righteously, like that settled it. He went back to shoveling spaghetti into his mouth. She found she didn't have an appetite anymore.

"What do you need the money for?" she asked, trying to be kind. It came across as condescending, but she couldn't help that. She knew her brother and he had his pride. He wouldn't ask for money, he'd come up with some way in which he was owed it and then get angry when he didn't get his perceived due. "You can tell me," she said, her voice deliberately light.

It didn't help.

"You miserable old hag," he yelled, jumping to his feet. "You've always done this. Always insisted I have less than you, that I'm constantly around you because I need a hand-out."

"You typically are," she shot back, completely confident in her assertion. But it was the wrong thing to say. He exploded with rage, ranting and raving about what was fair, pacing up and down the room. Eventually he ran out of steam, finally finishing off his now cold dinner.

They parted ways not an hour later, neither asking or offering for him to stay the night, though there was no doubt it would have been easier, it was very late now and the roads in that part of Tuscany were perilous and winding. He left one hundred euros richer, which was far more than he had earned, in her opinion.

She went to bed hungry that night, unable to face making anything else. Instead, she sighed into her pillow – she had been doing that a lot recently. To her dismay, she had learned why people in silly romance novels sighed so much. It was because there was an ache inside, a grief so overwhelming, so massive that it just had to be let out, the smallest drop allowed to spill from an overwhelming ocean of grief. For her, the only thing she could think to do was breathe, try to breathe through everything. Because as angry as she was, as scared as she was...she only really felt one emotion. She missed him. It was that pure and that simple. It did not abate.

Again, sleep did not go as well as she had hoped. The house creaked, as Mark had said it would. But it wasn't that that woke her.

It was a gentle, rhythmic sound. A familiar sound. *Thud, thud, thud*.

No house simply made that noise of its own accord! she thought, feeling the hysteria of the previous night consuming her again, the serenity of the morning totally gone. She buried her face in her pillow. It was not the whistling of the wind, or the creaking of the timber. It felt...deliberate.

Sometimes the noise would stop, just long enough for her to pray it was all over, before starting again.

It went on all night. All night, until the first rays of dawn crept into the room, birdsong taking over. She hadn't slept a wink, and she still had a full day's work to do.

She tried to sleep a little after dawn, hiding under the covers and pretending it was just a very bright night, as the sun flooded the curtainless windows. But it didn't work. She was awake now, mind clouded with worries.

So eventually, she got up, carrying Floppy down with her. She had this strange idea that if she just pretended everything was okay, committed fully to the bit, then she would *make* things okay, as if the universe just couldn't say no to her. It was important, like a badge of honor, that this didn't affect her at all. She wouldn't let it.

"The living room needs work," she said, putting him down against the window. She tried to master her breathing, but it took a long time to settle, as if she had just run a mile.

And so the day passed, and Greta hummed lightly to herself as she worked, trying to keep the fear – and its gruesome implications – at bay. She was successful too, just not for the reasons she had hoped. Around noon she started to unpack her first box of the day, desperately looking for more cooking supplies.

Instead, she found their wedding photos. Not only an album, puffy and white with a little sheer bow attached to the cover, but the huge prints she'd had made for their 50th anniversary.

How wonderful he looked, in his charcoal suit, pink orchid attached to his lapel, a jovial expression on his face. Her heart clenched. Once more looking around to check that no one was watching, she ran a hand across the photo, desperately trying to recall his touch.

It was hard, to be without him. It was hard every single day.

But still, she forced a smile onto her lips. She had looked beautiful that day. Stunning, in fact. She remembered how good she felt, how regal, how blessed. She still felt proud, looking at it now. She had such good taste. Her dress was timeless, not the tat other women wore, which now looked dated and ugly. No, her delicate silk dress with a sweetheart neckline and a hint of lace still looked fantastic. Timeless and classic. Not to mention the orchids and peonies she held in her hands – still so "in"! She was proud of that.

She hesitated. What should she do with the photos? Get rid of them? Would it be strange to hang them up, a constant reminder of what she had lost?

No, she decided, her jaw clenching. She wouldn't get rid of such loveliness, wouldn't forget *her* life just because it had him in it. She put the photos everywhere. Spread them out across the house, leaning them against window sills where she had not yet put tables. They made her forget, even for the briefest of milliseconds. They made her happy. And that she decided, was all that mattered.

Chapter Three

Weeks slowly crept by in this manner, with Greta's days spent working on the house and her nights spent fretting. Everynight now had those horrible sounds, the strange and intrusive demands for attention.

It was around three in the morning, a cold and unpleasant night, with rain slowly dripping down the windows and no moon to speak of, that a horrible realization struck her.

She was deaf. She wasn't supposed to be able to hear strange sounds in the middle of the night, certainly not distant creaking in a house this size. She could barely hear Davide when he came to chat, so how on earth...

Either she was making it up, going mad, all alone like this...Or there was something supernatural about the sounds, something that wanted to be heard, that knew how to get her attention. How else could she hear everything so acutely, with such aching detail? When usually she had to concentrate to understand anything at all? It had been years and years since her hearing was that good.

She shoved the fear deep down inside, determined not to be silly. But something was opening inside her, slowly. A dawning awareness that maybe, maybe she wasn't mad. Maybe there was something else. Watching her.

But yet again, it was as hard to be afraid in the cold light of day as it was to avoid being afraid at night. The sounds are strange, yes, but what can she do? Call someone and say she's hearing things? Oh, the horror! To hear things! They wouldn't understand. She'd be laughed out of the house. More to the point, who would she call? Frederick? She hadn't heard from him in five months. Her brother? No, for obvious reasons. That sweet neighbor? No, he already thought she was useless. Mary-Beth? Perhaps but she could do nothing, she was in hospital again with her hip.

Instead, she got a cat.

"I don't want a kitten," she had said firmly to the nice lady running the shelter. "Give me an older cat. Someone calmer. Someone that will like my lap."

That's exactly what she got. A gorgeously fluffy gray and white boy, with a ruff to rival a lion's and a quick purr. She immediately adored him.

"What's his name?" she asked, as he rubbed his face on hers.

"Delta," the woman said, "you know, like the Greek letter. Had a whole bunch of cats come in at once, you see and we just...ran down the alphabet."

"Delta," she said, looking into the cat's almond eyes, "Come and meet Floppy."

And it was as easy as that. Thankfully, they got along well, both sharing similar personality traits, such as having a predisposition to doing as little as possible.

The two of them helped her a lot, she wasn't ashamed to admit that. It helped that she had no one to admit it to, of course.

But she had a choice to make the first night Delta was home. Give into her fear and shut him in her room with her, or gamble that there was truly nothing sinister outside her room.

"I may be old, but I'm not a fool," she said, scratching the cat behind his ears. She had finally cleared the living room and paid some local teenagers to set up her new couch for her. The two of them were sprawled across it, Delta purring happily. She felt a lightness in her chest she had not experienced in a long time, looking down at his luscious belly and soft paws.

"Besides, you'd hate to be cooped up in my room all night, wouldn't you?" she cooed as he rubbed his face on her hand.

It was nice, having someone there. She felt content as she fell asleep that night, knowing in her heart of hearts that she would attribute any sound to the cat and therefore be less afraid.

But she hadn't counted on *that*.

She woke up to an ear-splitting scream. Wild and feral, the sound of someone truly in pain, a wordless plea for help so primal it was immediately understood, no matter who or what you were. Greta tore out of the room, skidding on the wood floors as she raced downstairs, the cat still wailing for its life.

She didn't even look, just grabbed wildly at him, gathering him in her arms and streaking upstairs again. She wasn't sure, but could have sworn she felt a breath at her neck, hot with a sweet smell. She felt her stomach drop.

But she didn't have time to pay attention. She raced to her room, feet skidding on the wooden floors, finally, desperately slamming the door shut. Only then did she stop to look at Delta.

He was panting, as if it was he that had been running, his eyes wide and staring. But he was alive. She sank to the bed, cursing herself for putting her in danger. And then she looked a little more closely.

His leg was hanging limply from the side of his body, at an unnatural angle no cat should ever have to endure. She gulped.

"I'm so sorry, pet." She gently put her head on his. He froze at first, his small body tense with anticipation, but eventually nuzzled her back. She let out a whimper, nausea curling in the pit of her stomach. All she wanted to do was hide.

But that would do neither of them any good. Heart hammering and with a determination she didn't know she possessed, she readied herself to leave the confines of her bedroom once more. She dressed quickly, paying little attention to the light yellow trousers and white top she threw on, gathering her things with a surprising ferocity, suddenly angry she had to put up with all this nonsense. It was with deliberate tenderness that she grabbed Delta, however. At first he purred, nuzzling into her chest and a satisfied wiggle. But that didn't last long.

When he saw where they were going he writhed and twisted, biting her hand with a strength she didn't know he had in him. Still, she held on, pushing down a grimace.

Holding her breath as if she were about to dive underwater, she sprinted out, up the hallway, down the stairs and, slamming into the front door, pushed it open with all her might. It took an agonizing few moments for it to open, old and heavy as it was. She had just one moment to look back down the hallway.

She wished she hadn't.

There, framed perfectly in the kitchen door, was a shadow. Unmistakably a woman, with thick skirts and a cane in one hand, it lumbered slowly towards her. Suddenly, Greta felt very cold. There was ice inside of her, a terrible ice that clawed at her stomach and wormed its way up her throat.

Finally wrestling the door open, she flung herself out, down the stairs and into her car at last. She sat there, letting herself breathe for a moment, before turning on the lights and heading out, faithfully following her GPS.

The emergency vet was almost an hour and a half away, and they cost a fortune. They also had a lot of questions for her, bringing in a cat she hadn't even owned for twenty four hours. Thankfully, they could see her genuine concern. And as most of them assumed she was just a doddery old lady, they didn't have the heart to take her cat away from her. To be fair to them, she did look rather pathetic. She was shaking, the terror of the night still clinging to her, almost visibly weighing her down. She couldn't focus at all when they asked her basic questions, could barely fill out the forms. Nothing seemed real, she half expected ghosts to pop out of the walls even here. Finally, she calmed herself, finished the forms, and waited.

Eventually the vet came to see her, a middle aged woman with thick, dark hair. "What happened?" Greta asked, arms wrapped around herself. "Do you know? Because I – I don't. I was just asleep and then I heard him crying. And I found him like this." She explained in a rush.

"Well," the vet said, petting Delta softly. "There are lots of reasons a cat might dislocate a hip, such as a fall from a great height or perhaps a congenital disorder. Did the shelter mention anything about that when you adopted him?"

"No, they didn't have any records. He was found on the street. They think he must have been an indoor cat before that, but..." she shrugged. "They just found him. No idea who the previous owners might have been." She bit her lip, praying there would be an easy answer.

"Sadly that's not uncommon. We've checked him for a chip and he doesn't have one, so...he's all yours I guess," the vet said with a shrug, looking fondly down at Delta. It was hard not to get attached to this soft ball of gray.

"So," Greta said, trying to sound casual. "This...this is normal for cats?" God how she hoped so. For a single mad moment, she imagined the vet would say something like 'oh yeah, cats often make people hallucinate ghosts and ghoulies, but no worries! That's totally normal' She didn't, of course, she didn't say anything like that.

Instead she simply smiled and shrugged. "Normal enough. Cats get into strange things sometimes. Is there anything he could have fallen from?"

"I do have stacks of boxes almost to the ceiling in that room. He might have been playing perhaps, or exploring..."

She kept nodding. "Yes, yes, all sounds very possible. Cats are curious creatures. Especially if he smelled something. Well. Try to move the boxes as quickly as possible. Hopefully it won't happen again." Greta smiled, palpable relief washing through her. Yes. Yes, it really was that simple. An expert had told her so. Who was she to doubt that? She thanked everyone at the clinic profusely, silently vowing to send flowers later. They deserved it, helping a mad old woman at three o'clock in the morning.

Finally, they got back in the car, Delta's little leg bandaged up. She let out a long, shaky breath. They were okay. Everything was okay.

"I think we will be staying in the hotel tonight," she said softly. A strange part of her wished she'd bought Floppy with them, worried now that anything she held dear would be a target.

But a target for what? Her stomach roiled uneasily. For the first time she noticed her shoulders were tense, hunched up by her ears, and that her back was aching. Dully, she wondered how long they had been that way. With a deep breath, she pushed them down.

She couldn't think. She had to rest. It suddenly seemed as if an age had passed since she had truly been able to sit down in peace. She followed her phone to the nearest hotel and booked a room. She didn't dare ask if Delta was allowed, fearing that the answer would be a resounding no, and simply smuggled him in under her jacket. For the first time in what felt like ages, she slept the whole night through. It was blissful.

But she knew that eventually she would have to return to the house. The hotel was a brief reprieve, not a solution.

She stopped the car at the base of her driveway, looking up at the Victorian mansion. It was stunning. Even with the garden so thoroughly overgrown, even with the roof missing some tiles, even with thousands of tiny problems, she could see how beautiful it was.

She carried Delta in and placed him gently on the couch, glad to see he didn't seem to have any residual fear of his environment. Perhaps he really had fallen?

But that woman...she knew what she had seen. There was no denying it now. But it was so hard. It was so hard to trust herself, when the house was this big, when she was so used to consulting others for advice. Still, even the memory of the shadow made her cold, a faint shiver running down her spine. But she couldn't live in denial any longer. Ignoring things was perfectly acceptable, even enjoyable, until it started to harm those you held dear. Tormenting her was one thing, but not Delta. He was too important.

"I suppose...the first problem..." she said slowly, testing out each of the words, "would be...to isolate what the problem truly is." But how do you measure coincidences? How do you verify accidents?

She leant back on the couch, looking up at the marvelous frescos.

She knew what she was trying to say, although she found that she was too ashamed to say it, even to Delta. This was, she had to admit, something more. Some strange spirits or demons or- she didn't even know what. But something was here. There was no denying it now.

She had always been agnostic. Though she had scoffed at crystals and charlatans, she had flirted with tarot readings and such in her youth. It wasn't entirely out of the realm of possibility for her, that maybe, maybe there was something beyond. In fact, she had once felt certain of it, felt certain her life was so blessed, so good that she must be a favorite of the gods (or fate, or spirits, she had never really decided).

But at the same time, she knew how insane it would sound. Her cat had an accident. Ancient pipes don't always work correctly. One room was colder than another. And that was enough to make her think she had a ghost? People would laugh their heads off if they knew she was even contemplating it.

But they didn't have to know. Wasn't that one of the joys, maybe the only joy, of living alone? She didn't have anyone to impress.

She looked down at Delta's leg and sighed. She couldn't risk not taking the events of the previous night seriously. She owed that to him.

So that day, she did two things.

Firstly, she phoned the priest. This was a hard needle to thread. She certainly wasn't ready to tell him the whole story. What she did say was that she needed God's blessing. She mumbled something about 'feeling the devil' and then just pretended to be deaf when he asked follow up questions. She quite enjoyed that bit. Still, he agreed to come. She had a feeling that perhaps he didn't have a lot to do around here.

"Please bless this room only," she said, leading him into the dining room. "I'm not sure if you can control it like that, but, well..."

He smiled indulgently at her. "Of course." Then, after throwing around some holy water and muttering some Latin, off he went. Didn't make her feel much better, and she privately felt that she could have done all that herself, but it was at least a start.

Secondly, the salt. She didn't remember where she had heard about this. Perhaps it was a stupid old wives' tale, perhaps it was something she had seen on TV or in a fantasy novel. But she had always had a vague idea that salt was protective in some way. That demons don't like it – or maybe it was witches? Something like that, anyway. The next room she cleaned, the last on the ground floor, she dosed with a generous mixture of salt and water, keeping her fingers crossed just in case that helped.

Then she took both Floppy and Delta to bed with her, shutting the door firmly behind them.

That night was the worst yet.

It started with a creaking. Then the *Thud, thud, thud* came back – always that strange, halting rhythm. Closer it seemed this time, so close it made Delta's fur stand on end, hissing in a way she'd never seen a cat do before.

Her heart hammered in her chest, her limbs suddenly numb with fear. It was then that the door knob began to turn. She launched herself at the door, holding it firm. It pushed back. She could feel it try to open, as if something on the other side was leaning against it. She knew she couldn't hold out long; her socked feet were already slipping on the wooden floors.

God, how she wished she had someone there to help her.

But she didn't.

So she reached out, grabbed one of her moving boxes and used it to hold the door shut. Her bones ached, profoundly unused to such a task. Her joints screamed at her, begging her to stop, but she simply couldn't. She kept going, adding another, and another, until finally none of them moved. Until the barricade was so strong, nothing could get in. The *Thud, thud, thud* moved away slowly, presumably retreating down the long corridor.

She took a long, deep breath, for what felt like the first time in a long time. Her heart began to slow to its normal pace, her knees giving way as she dropped slowly to the floor. She was safe. For tonight at least, she was safe. Finally, she crawled back into bed, cuddling Delta and Floppy close, swearing to keep them safe.

The next day was odd. She found that she didn't really want to leave her room, not even in daylight. Up until now her fears had seemed stupid and unfounded when looked at critically. Now, things were different. Now she knew.

Nothing could turn a door handle – nothing except a hand. She knew what she felt, knew that there had to be something- or someone- trying to open it.

She wanted to reach out to Frederick. Even if he didn't love her anymore, he had always been a wise and sensible man. He would be a good friend in this, she knew. And, bizarrely, she knew if she cared a little bit less, if she wasn't still holding a candle for him, she probably could. But her love was so obvious, so impossible to hide, that it would simply be a pathetic ex-wife, making up any excuse to talk to her beloved once more.

Finally, she forced herself out of bed, Delta needed breakfast after all.

What she saw downstairs removed any doubt in her mind about just how bad the situation was.

It was like a tornado had ripped through the house, ripping security cameras down, chucking pillows about, her wedding photos all askew, the dining room where the priest had been was hit worst of all, the chairs in disarray.

But the salt room was untouched. Amazingly, wonderfully, fabulously, untouched. She couldn't help it, she let out a whoop of joy, clapping her hands together. She had figured something out. Not all of it, not even close. But something. The salt made things safe. She had done *something*. She mattered.

She raced out to town, buying out multiple shops' worth of salt. Her car was packed full of it, so much that it exhausted her trying to carry all of it in, having to take breaks and even leave some there. Maybe it would stop her car from being haunted anyway.

It was only when she sat down to lunch that she truly considered what all this might mean.

What could it possibly be? A ghost? A poltergeist? What was the difference between the two, anyway? And what is this logic behind the salt?

She picked up Floppy and squeezed him tight. "So if I accept, if I really accept, that this is supernatural. What does that mean?" It means there's an afterlife, she realized, looking into his big black eyes. It means that death, which seemed so close to her now, was not the end. She didn't know how to feel about that. She thought of her parents, who she still missed every day. Her little sister, who died when they were just children. She had always hoped that heaven was real, but only in the same sort of way you hope for world peace or a cure for cancer. Yes, it would be nice, but you're not planning your whole life around it.

Now... should she go to church more? She scoffed at this idea, the priest had clearly been useless. Worse than that, he had seemed antagonistic. Besides, she just didn't see why Christianity would be the answer above so many other valid philosophies. No, she highly doubted that was it.

But what then? She pondered the question all day, as she scrubbed yet another room down with her 'magic elixir'. She was far more confident this time, feeling a surge of pride and protectiveness. She would make this house beautiful again, she would. She promised herself that.

So it was with a sense of stubborn pride that she opened one more box.

For just a moment, her smile slipped. Her knitting things. She had only ever made gifts for others, not once for herself. And she felt no remorse about that -- there was a genuine joy in giving. But she had forgotten. She had forgotten she took some back. In a moment of righteous indignation she had ripped Fredrick's sweaters from the hangers, declaring that she had made them and therefore she could take them.

They still smelled like him. She lifted a jumper to her face and sighed. For just one moment she fooled herself; the memories were so strong, so welcome, it was almost like he was back.

Not only that, but it was a beautifully made jumper. With two cables down the front and a pattern of seed stitch on the sleeves, there wasn't a single mistake in the whole thing. It had been his favorite.

"I made it." She said defensively. Floppy just sat there. "I can do what I want with it."

So she did. She positioned it artfully across a chair, as if it had just been flung there, its owner planning on coming back and claiming it in just a moment. Artificially casual. It made her smile. And besides, no one else had to know. She did the same with the various scarves she made, hanging them up by the door, just the way he used to like. And the gloves too, shoved in the second drawer to the right, so he would know where to find them. Like nothing had changed.

After yet another disappointing dinner, she returned to her room, heaping a large line of salt outside the door, hoping it would protect the threshold. This time, she said a prayer too. Not to any deity in particular, more to the earth itself. She had no idea if this did any good or not, but still. She doubted it would hurt.

She went to bed, desperate for morning to come.

Chapter Four

Remarkably, it did. Still, the thudding came. Still the house creaked. And this time, there was a faint crying to be heard, like a young woman in need of help. But her door remained untouched, as did the salted rooms.

She suddenly felt powerful.

With a flash of inspiration, Delta had rock salt hot glued onto his collar. "I'm lucky I got such a good boy." She cooed as she attached it. "Not many cats would put up with this." She said, as he lolled about happily on her bed. Oh to have a man easily satisfied! To have someone look adoringly up at you for simply being you! To love and to be loved! It was a joy. She suddenly wondered how she had ever lived without a cat in her life.

Floppy was taken down to the sea, dipped in and carefully left to dry in the sun. Its salinity would be sufficient, and besides, she had not visited it yet. It was beautiful. A tiny pebble beach with high rocky cliffs and the purest blue waters. It took her breath away with its sheer majesty, it gave her some sort of comfort to know that it wasn't only ghosts that endure the test of time, but nature and beauty too.

She spent a relaxing afternoon there. She wasn't quite happy enough to be alone with her thoughts yet, but she had bought a good book, and easily got lost in it. A nice change. Suddenly she vowed to try harder, to try and make herself happy. It was clear no one else was going to try.

So she was surprised to return home to see a man standing on her porch.

"Davide," she said, impressed at herself for remembering the neighbor's name. She silently felt she deserved some recognition for that.

"Hi," he said, beaming at her, a rather large package in his hands. "I hope you're doing well!"

"Well enough..." she said, then worried about how bland this sounded. "And yourself?"

"Oh fine, fine. You know I was talking to my husband the other day about this house – I really have always admired it you know – and he reminded me that we actually had the original curtains in our basement. So I thought I'd bring them over." He said, nodding towards the box. "See if you want them."

"Oh how lovely!" She said, a genuine smile cracking across her face. "However did you get them?"

"Well, we actually have quite a lot of stuff. When that family moved in, the one in the 60's... The Gallo's, I think their name was. Anyway, when they moved in, they removed a lot of this kind of thing, just threw it out. My family has always been a bit uh...magpie-ish, shall we say. Anything historic, you know. Always worth saving. I think my mother intended to make a dress out of these, but never quite got around to it. So it's just been sitting in our storage for ages. And I thought, well, why not return it? It is good, I think, to care for old things, you know?"

"Of course," Greta said, still smiling. "Why don't you come in for some tea? I've got it all a bit more organized now."

As Davide came in, he marveled at everything about the house, from the orange carvings on the banister, to the quality of the marble fireplaces, and the unique beauty of the frescos. Together, they admired it all. They were having such a good time and it was so nice to have company that when he offered to help her put the curtains up, she didn't even hesitate. And when he stayed around to clean, it just seemed natural.

It was only when the sun was setting and she was tucking Floppy into bed next to her that she realized – she had forgotten to salt the room.

She groaned, knowing what that meant. Re-doing the whole thing tomorrow. She sighed as she spritzed down her own door, as she knew would become her habit. Oh well, at least she was moderately confident that the three of them were safe inside and would actually live to see the dawn. That was enough.

She actually found she was getting used to the creaking and the thudding, accepting them as parts of the house, supernatural or otherwise. It felt, strangely, like company. She knew she must be losing her mind, but sometimes, when the thudding didn't come for longer than usual, she worried about it. Hoped it was okay.

"How pitiful have I become?" she asked the stuffed toy next to her. "Worrying about the sound?"

She did though, and secretly, she wasn't as ashamed of it as she thought she would be. Presumably the thing had some sort of consciousness. If it was supernatural, a fact she was *almost* ready to accept. And if it did, presumably it felt loneliness and pain just as much as she did? Presumably it...wanted something? She wondered idly if she should try and do a burial, or even a ritual. She'd heard about that, of course. The classic ghost stories where souls could not rest in peace until...something something.

But having no answers and seeing no point in worrying, she put the question out of her mind, determined to sleep.

It was with a well rested but profound resignation that she stepped into the drawing room the next day, feeling certain she'd know what she would find.

But it was fine. The curtains, red velvet crossed with silver thread, a gossamer layer of mint green beneath, still hung proudly on their silver rods. The room was neat and tidy. No damage at all. Seemingly.

She was suspicious.

It felt like a trap or a trick. As if it, the strange creature that haunted this house, were saying "sure, you can put your guard down. The salt isn't necessary, I'll play nice!" She wasn't buying it. But she was grateful not to have to do the work again and so, as some sort of compromise, she left that room alone for the rest of the day, mentally declaring it a truce. A no man's land.

Instead, deciding that her walk to the sea yesterday had done her good, she struck out into the garden, shocked at herself that she hadn't explored it yet.

It was truly stunning.

It was overgrown of course, and would probably need an entire team of gardeners to get it into shape, but still. She could imagine what it must have looked like in its glory days.

Roses were everywhere, bursting with pops of color. Pink here, yellow there, even deep purple. Not to mention the sheer variety of other flowers that had taken over. Grape hyacinths were everywhere, weed-like in their abundance. Crocuses popped out of the ground, nestled between ferns and ivy. Trees towered above them, offering shade and comfort, an ancient wrought iron bench sitting prettily between two of the tallest.

And of course, the maze. That was what really got Greta's attention. It was still astonishing how large her land was, there was no way she could have afforded this if it wasn't in such disrepair.

She made her way over, beating a path to it through the unkempt grass, head full of fantasies of what this could become- what she could make it. The structure of the maze was still strikingly sound, impressively so, considering how little attention it had been given. No, she wouldn't change that at all. She was too impressed by its tenacity. But she wanted more fruits, liked the idea of abundance and growth. Perhaps a pear tree, or maybe even cherry. Yes, she decided, proud of herself for thinking of it. Bright red cherries. Then she could bake with them as well, make delicious goodies out of delightful colors.

With her head so full of fantasies, it was no surprise, really, when she fell. She hit the ground hard, her knees first and then her wrists, pain shooting up through all her joints.

"Sod it," she admonished herself, "you silly old fool." She stood and brushed herself off, dirt covering her once white trousers. Her ankle stung particularly, and her heart sank at the idea it might be sprained. How would she manage with only one hand? The thought filled her with dread. And with that she hobbled back inside. Getting lost in a maze was too much for her today.

Besides, she did have work to do, still, and she threw herself at the second floor bathroom with righteous vigor. She would regret it the next day, clearly she had fallen harder than she thought. Her ankle had swelled to almost twice its size, throbbing with pain. Despite that, she still tried to soldier on, it was well past noon by the time she finally gave up and admitted defeat.

She dragged herself to the doctor of course, enduring their pitying looks and sanctimonious sighs. But all they had to say was that falls happen, especially at her age, be careful, especially at her age, and that she might want some help around the house – especially at her age. Useful, she sneered to herself as she drove home, the vineyards of Tuscany whizzing past her car window.

All the doctor had recommended was a splint and bed. And so she resigned herself to spending the next few days at rest, alone with her thoughts.

It was awful. She missed him, so much. He was supposed to be there. He always used to take care of her when she was sick, always made sure she was okay. She clung to Floppy even more than usual in those days, literally pushing him into her stomach so it wouldn't hurt quite as much. She found that with no distractions, the ache came back with a vengeance. The pain had never got better, exactly. But she had begun to create a life around it. To have other things to fill her time with. Now, with the enforced rest, all that was gone. Only he remained, vivacious and alive in her memories. She couldn't seem to stop, all other options for entertainment, or distraction or even just mental rest seemed closed to her now. All she could do was think, and wait, and fret. Worst of all, she found that since she didn't have the opportunity to exhaust herself during the day, she didn't sleep well at night.

She did manage to finally have a nice dinner. She tricked herself into doing it, of course. She made Frederick's favorite meal, Bistecca alla Fiorentina, slipping easily into a fantasy that she was making it for him. That he would be home anytime soon. Pushing herself to make it good enough to serve someone else.

It was excellent, the steak rich and flavorful, the olive oil well-balanced and complex. She wondered idly why she never bothered to put that much effort into cooking for herself, why she pretended to be content with spaghetti attacked by tinned asparagus (an abomination no true Italian would endure). She had no answers for that.

STRANGE AND TWISTED THINGS 45

That night, she dozed fitfully, lying awake and listening to the strange sounds of the house. There wasn't any rhythm to the creaks and thuds that she could riddle out. The crying was becoming worse. She had a theory that this too was a manipulation, a ploy to get her to come out of her room and try and save some helpless soul. She was tempted, she had to admit. Whatever was out there, it was cunning.

Greta did, of course, spend some time trying to figure out the source of the sound. But in her mental state, she wasn't sure if that was wise. She had always been a somewhat obsessive person. She liked to dive deep into projects, or ideas, or, sadly, people, and give herself to them fully. After only one day of googling things like "Why don't demons like salt?" and "Are curses real?", she knew she was worrying herself far more than the demon (or ghost, or poltergeist, or fey, or wandering spirit, or...) actually had. The things she read were wild, and worse, contradictory. She would latch onto ideas and simply feel unable to let go, doing mad things like leaving a jar of water open under the full moon (she actually hadn't totally given up on this one) or ordering kilos of garlic to her house, though even she couldn't quite stretch her imagination to vampires.

Her body rested, even if her mind did not. It just didn't seem to be healing.

"Well, I guess that's to be expected, at my age," she muttered to Floppy. "I just can't believe I was so stupid."

Listless and bored, she would look down at her ankle almost obsessively, as if she could wish it better. It was looking a bit...odd. It was swollen, but instead of going red, it was faintly darker. Bruising, she expected. Although wouldn't that be in lumps and shapes, not the entire thing, not slowly creeping up her leg....? She didn't know. Couldn't know, as no doctor would take her seriously, and Google was a nightmare of answers from "It's certainly cancer" to "You're going crazy" and "It's a demon" (a suggestion she found far less humorous than she would have just a few short months ago). Finally she just gave up, deciding that at her age, she had enough aches and pains to be getting on with, one more probably wouldn't hurt.

So the days passed by, Davide occasionally dropping more things off, everything from random, mismatched pillows to positively ancient kitchenware, anything that was even vaguely related to the house. It made her smile. She wouldn't say she was happy, but she was adapting. She could feel it: with each room cleaned and wall washed she felt the pain coming out of her, turning into love, creating something wonderful. *She knew eventually, better times would come. This too shall pass, after all.*

And slowly, her home was becoming everything she loved. Antiques filling the rooms, velvet pillows strewn about. She even managed to find an old grandfather clock exactly like the one she used to have. She told herself that it was the same one, that Fredrick probably threw it out (he always hated it) and that it had ended up at an estate sale in her new town. She smiled, deciding that it was fate that had reunited them.

Greta loved every single thing in that house, unashamedly. She was quickly learning to truly enjoy being alone, to let her obsessions rush out of her in waves. She had even started drawing again, like she used to, recreating one of their wedding photos in charcoal. It bought her such joy, to study that face over and over again. It was almost like he was back. She should have taken more time, she admonished herself, to study him while he was still there.

So it was with decidedly mixed feelings that she answered the phone one day to find her old friend Mary-Beth on the other end.

"Hello dear!" she called out jovially.

"Mary B. I haven't heard from you in weeks. How are you?" Greta asked, idly lighting a rose and cedarwood candle (they had always had such candles in their home, and she would be damned if she stopped now).

"Never been better. Well, apart from all my ailments." She then went straight on to name a very long list of them. "But enough about me. I've been thinking about you a lot recently. Thought I should check in. How's the new house?"

Greta desperately scrambled for something to say. "It...takes some getting used to, living like this. But. It is beautiful here. Part of me does love it, you know, even if it wasn't my first choice."

"I'm so glad." Mary-Beth sighed. "You know, I was wondering if I could come and see it? You're about halfway between me and my niece, and I thought, well why not make a visit out of it?"

"Of course!" Greta called out, already thinking of which dinner plates to use. The one with the golden Greek fret pattern. It had been her wedding set and it would be nice to get it out again.

"I could spend a few nights–" Mary-Beth twittered away, excitement evident in her voice.

"When are you thinking of coming?" Greta spoke over her, before she had really processed what the other woman had said.

"Maybe next week? Saturday to Monday? If it wouldn't be a bother?" Mary-Beth sounded nervous, despite their many years of friendship. She had never been one to intrude and still carried around a small sense of guilt with her, as if she was asking for too much.

"Of course! Absolutely!" Greta gushed. She wouldn't dream of turning a friend away, even if it was 'too much'. "I'd love to see you!" And then she froze. Could she really have a guest, here? At night? She had never done that before. And she could hardly lock Mary-Beth in her room, could she?

"But, ah, you see Mary –" She started.

"Oh thank you, I'm so excited!" Mary jabbered on. "You know I haven't seen you in months! It will be good to catch up."

"Well, yes, but –" she tried in vain.

"And besides – oh gosh, that's the doorbell, I have to dash, could be the repairman I've been waiting for. But I'll text you!" And with that she hung up the phone.

Greta gulped. Could she offer to get her friend a hotel? Claim her home wasn't habitable yet? Or maybe that her leg was too hurt? But no, Mary-Beth would only worry, offer to come down and take care of her. Or worse yet, tell her brother.

They did text about it, Greta using every excuse in the book, but not quite able to say no. She couldn't bear the thought of rejecting the woman outright; Mary-Beth always took it so poorly, so personally, it actually seemed preferable to risk the ghosts than let her down. Besides, it had been so long since they had seen each other...

Instead, she told herself that she had the house under control. That the salt was enough. That really nothing horrific had happened, apart from the flooding in the kitchen, the devastation that had followed the blessing, her cat being injured, the non stop noises at night – really, it was all perfectly fine. She had lived in this house for weeks before she was able to fully accept the possibility that it might be, well, haunted. She still couldn't quite accept the word, even now. Mary-Beth would be fine for a single night.

And so, Saturday arrived – as did her first overnight guest.

Chapter Five

Mary-Beth was sweet as ever, trotting up to greet Greta with a hug. They had been friends since their school days, both having arrived in Italy as young girls, knowing little of the language or customs. They had faced this strange new country together, sharing their dismay at the grammar, so foreign to both English and German, and their wonder at the breadth of Italy's history and culture. By now, of course, they felt truly Italian. But it had been a long road, and they were both glad they hadn't had to do it alone.

Mary-Beth was appropriately amazed at the house, oohing and ahhing at all the right spots. It wasn't incredibly old for Italy of course, where a hundred-and-fifty years seemed almost trivial. But it was like living in a museum: everywhere you looked, there was something worthy of respect. She was proud of it.

"So, how can I help?" Mary-Beth asked, looking around at the boxes that were still piled around.

"Oh, nonsense!" Greta countered, "Let's go out to the garden, relax a bit."

They sat on the sunny bench, laughing and joking, just like the old days. It was so nice, so strange for Greta to have company that she didn't notice how late it was getting, not until there was a chill in the air and the sun was just slipping behind the trees.

For the first time that day, she was worried.

"Let's go inside," she said, standing abruptly. Her knees objected to this sudden sensation, but she didn't have time to think about that now.

Mary-Beth dawdled, of course. She always took her time, and besides, to her the sunset was simply beautiful, a thing to be admired and applauded, and not a harbinger of something more.

"Now," Greta said, trying to keep her voice light and airy. After a long moment, Mary-Beth finally stood, letting herself be led back to the house.

"I don't know about you, but I'm tired." Greta said, her mouth suddenly dry. She looked across at her friend, as if only now realizing what she had done. What she had exposed her to.

"I uh, I would appreciate it if you would not leave your room at night. It's very…dark here. And uh. The floor creaks. A lot. Any sound you make will echo through the whole house. Sounds most strange! And uh, please do forgive me if you hear me crying at night," she said, in a flash of inspiration. "It's just hard, you know. Without Frederick."

"Of course –"

"And if you see salt, that's just for the bugs," she said, her voice rising. She had never lied to Mary-Beth like this before.

"Bugs?" her friend asked, head cocked to one side.

"Yes, I've heard it, uh, it's bad for them. They don't like it. Anyway! Please do remember what I said. Don't leave your room for any reason tonight. Bedtime!" And with that, she turned on her heel, leading her friend up the stairs and to her room.

"It's not much, I'm afraid." Greta wished she had thought to bring in some flowers. The room was lined with shelves, filled with nothing but a few knick-knacks and her old wedding photos. but was otherwise quite bare – she guessed that once it had been used as a library.

One day, she would bring it back to its former glory, she vowed. Now it was just so empty. A fold out couch sat in the middle of the room, made up with soft blue linen. That at least, was nice, the pillows new and fluffy, the sheets tucked in.

"Oh, it's lovely. Again, thank you so much for having me," Mary-Beth said with a hug. "I uh – I'm surprised to see…" she started, gesturing to a snapshot of Greta and Fredrick cutting the cake.

"Now. Remember what I said about the house…" Greta reminded her, blushing deeply.

Mary-Beth assured her, repeatedly, that she did, and besides, she was so tired anyway she would probably be able to sleep through a herd of elephants.

Greta sighed as she closed the door behind her, giving it one last spritz of salt water before heading to bed herself, praying she had done the right thing.

She couldn't sleep that night and, honestly, she hadn't really expected to, not when she was so worried about her friend. Whereas last night the thumping had become so familiar it faded into the background, now it seemed sharp and sinister, seen fresh again from her friend's perspective.

And then the crying started. In truth it didn't sound like Greta at all: far too high pitched, more like a young girl's voice than an old woman's. She just prayed Mary-Beth was asleep.

It was around three in the morning when she heard a door open. It was so loud that even Delta perked his head up, resentfully awakened from a deep snooze. Her heart leapt into her mouth. Was that Mary-Beth, up and awake? Or was it…something else? Perhaps something trying to trick her into leaving the safety of her room? With trembling knees she got out of bed, pressing her ear against the door.

Footsteps, slow and uneven. But that could be anything, anyone. She tried to look through the keyhole, but it was so dark it told her nothing. She slipped her phone out of her pocket, hands shaking as she typed.

"Are you awake?" She heard the ping as the text message arrived at her friend's phone next door.

No response. Had she left it behind when she went to the bathroom, or –

A scream, human this time.

Greta yanked open the door, dashed out into the hallway. There, not four feet from her, stood her friend, and just behind her...something else. A tall figure, and yet just a shadow, no face to speak of but undeniable, red eyes. It reached out, one wispy hand trailing around Mary's neck. Mary's eyes went wide, too wide, as if they were about to pop out of her head. She clawed at her throat, desperately trying to get the thing off her but finding nothing solid, experiencing only a crushing weight and a desperate fight to breathe.

Greta gasped. She had never in her life seen anything so horrible – never felt so cold, so profoundly, overwhelmingly helpless.

Not knowing what else to do, Greta took her spray bottle and hurled it. It hit the ground and exploded, salt water going everywhere. The shadow reared back, releasing Mary-Beth for just a moment. That's all she needed.

She sprinted forward, practically throwing herself down the spiral staircase, taking the steps two at a time, the shadow in hot pursuit. They slammed the front door behind them, Greta taking the time to lock it, Mary-Beth leaving her and sprinting to her car. She flicked on the lights and sped away like a bat out of hell, tires screeching.

Greta wasn't far behind, she raced over to her car, throwing open the doors, intent on following her friend. But a thought stopped her.

Had she closed her bedroom door? Was Delta exposed to the shadow, the flimsy salted shield now gone? Or worse, had his cat-like innocence encouraged him to leave his sanctuary and explore?

She bit her lip. On the one hand, he was generally sedentary enough to avoid such excursions, but on the other...well. He was still a cat. She had already put him in harm's way once. She couldn't do it again. But how could she go inside?

And then she saw something that made her heart skip a beat. On the back seat, one final bag of salt she hadn't had the energy to bring inside yet. She grabbed it, knowing what she had to do. Heading back into the house, taking small handfuls of it and hurling it in front of her, she carefully made her way back to her room, and shut the door, cat happily inside, unaware there had even been a problem at all.

She still didn't sleep that night, but that was because she was mentally composing her apology to Mary-Beth. She would call her in the morning, she decided. She just hoped she could be forgiven. She didn't think she could stand to lose her husband and best friend in the same year. It would be too much.

And so it was with great surprise that she found the woman on her doorstep the next morning, holding the newspaper and looking sheepish.

"Sorry about last night," she said, sitting down on the swinging love seat that was suspended just outside the door.

"Oh Mary B, you don't have anything to apologize for," Greta said with relief, joining her. Suddenly, everything felt wrong. The air was too pleasant for this conversation, the cushions too plush, the sun too bright. Surely they should be inside, in some dusty corner? At the very least, it should be raining. That would be far more appropriate for a conversation about....all this.

"No, I was an old fool and I know it. And we always promised each other we would never become that. I just thought I heard something. Or felt something." Mary-Beth looked down at her knees.

"I...I think you might have." Greta said softly, biting her lip. Perhaps too softly, because her friend didn't seem to answer, prattling on by herself instead.

"I mean you warned me," Mary-Beth said with a light laugh. "You said, strange noises. 'Don't let it get to you, Mary B.' I thought you were just being your usual self about it, but no. I can really see how this place gets to you at night. Not at all like that this morning though, is it? It's....serene." She said, closing her eyes and leaning her head back, waves just audible in the far distance.

"I..." Greta started, swallowing hard. "I uh, I think you might be right, actually. About, uh...last night. I...I guess, what I mean to say is," and here she swallowed, struggling to force the words out, "I think the house is haunted."

"What?" Mary B said, sniggering, sure it was one of her jokes.

Finally, Greta told her everything. Every single strange occurrence and odd happening, she laid out bare before her friend. To her credit, Mary-Beth didn't laugh.

Wow," she said, after a long pause. "I have to say... this is a little concerning."

"I know," Greta said simply, looking up at the bright blue sky.

"I know it's new to you, living alone..." Mary started again, biting her lip.

"What?"

"You were with Frederick so long. I know it must be hard. I mean look how I reacted last night and I've been living on my own for over five years now! So...so I can really see why you read so much into these things. Truly, I do." Mary-Beth said, giving her hand a quick squeeze.

"It's – look, I'm telling you. The salt, it works." She insisted.

This only made her friend look more concerned.

"And, listen. There's even a mysterious door in the basement I can't open. Is there anything more 'classic haunted house' than that?" She asked, her shoulders suddenly tense. She knew how difficult this was to accept, but really. They had been best friends for decades, didn't that earn her a little trust?

"Well" Mary-Beth said slowly "Have you tried the keys the realtor gave you?"

Greta blushed. "I haven't got around to it yet." She muttered. In truth she'd been too afraid to go into the basement alone. Perhaps it was she being an old fool, but it was different down there. Damp, and dark.

Mary smiled softly. "Well, why don't we try together, hmm? And then we can have a look at some of your other problems." Greta gulped, the knot in her stomach untying itself. She trusted Mary-Beth above all else. Even above Frederick, now. If she said it was all in her head... well, maybe she was the one who should be more trusting, less stubborn.

"I guess I have been under a lot of stress recently. Everything is so different." She leaned against her friend, putting her head on her shoulder, inhaling her warm perfume.

"I know it must be," Mary-Beth said warmly. "I should stay a little longer, I think. Two more nights maybe? This is such a big house for one person..."

"That's what Frederick said," and she smiled at the memory, one of their last conversations together. "I think he thought I was trying to rip him off, get every last penny out of him. But...oh, I don't know. I wanted to take something old and forgotten and make it beautiful again. I wanted... a legacy, I suppose. I wanted something to be better, because I was here." And there her voice broke. She squeezed her eyes shut, praying Mary-Beth would leave her to her pride and not comment on such a stupid, foolish wish.

"My life is better because you are here," She cooed, not unlike how Greta would talk to her cat. But she didn't mind. Mary-Beth always knew exactly what to say.

They stayed like that for a while, until her friend finally said: "Come on, let's get this sorted out."

They stood up slowly, taking in one last lungful of fresh air before heading into the musty basement.

"Wooooooo...." Mary-Beth said, doing her best imitation of a ghost. Greta couldn't help but smile. She still held on tight to the banister as they descended the stairs, but, really it wasn't so bad. She reached over and clicked on the only light, necessary even in the daylight, and that made it even better.

She hadn't been afraid the first time she came down here, she remembered, and there was no need to be now. She didn't think she was crazy, logically speaking. But it was so hard to actually believe yourself, to trust your own senses when you knew the whole world would disagree. She swallowed hard.

"Let's open this door then." Mary Beth said, holding her hand out for the keys. *Fine*, Greta wanted to scream. *Prove that I'm mad, that I've been ruined, used and abandoned. That I have been pushed too far, pushed to a place normal people don't go, that I am, deep down inside, broken. That I'd rather live with ghosts and demons than live alone. Fine. Prove it to me.*

As she passed them over, her hand was shaking, a fact she tried in vain to hide.

"It's cold down here," Greta explained, though she knew a pre-emptive excuse made her seem even more guilty. She just didn't know what to think, didn't know what to do. And it was breaking her. She suddenly felt so foolish, so small and stupid.

Mary-Beth took the keys, turning to the door without a word. And that's when the lights went out. The bulb exploded, one bright flash of light before total darkness.

And then those eyes, bright and starring out of a featureless face. Her whole body went numb, a scream ripping its way through her body. For just one horrible second Greta stared at it, and it stared back, as if it could look into her very soul. And then she ran. She flew up the stairs, only one thought in her mind – get to the light.

She could hear Mary-Beth close behind her, she prayed it was her breath she felt, warm and wet on her neck, and not something worse. She was almost to the door, hand just grazing the doorknob when there was an almighty crash.

Mary-Beth had fallen, hitting every stair on the way down and collapsing into a heap on the basement floor. The eyes stood over her, something like a smile playing around them. Greta charged forward, racing to the kitchen, grabbing the salt. Praying it would work yet again.

She tore back to the top of the basement stairs, throwing it down as far as she could. It landed in soft arcs, like snow, each grain scattered delicately, uselessly. Far too thin a spread to be effective, not getting close enough to have any real effect. What's more, the eyes seemed to be ready for it now. A faint breeze emanated from it, waving away the grains and pushing them back up to her. It took its time, aware she was mesmerized, seeming to enjoy this show of strength and intelligence. It seemed that it wanted her to watch, wanted her to know, to be scared.

Slowly, delicately, it bent low over Mary-Beth, one hand curled around her face, tilting her up. Greta wanted to sob, but she knew she didn't have time. Instead she plunged her hand into her pocket, hands trembling over her phone as she desperately tried to turn on the flashlight.

A weak beam shot down the stairs. It wasn't enough. The eyes blinked, jumping slightly. It didn't seem to like the light particularly. But that was all. It wrapped a hand around her neck, squeezing once more, Mary Baths body trembling, squeezing, kicking out against nothing.

Greta would have to get closer. Light held in front of her like a shield, she crept down the stairs, legs trembling. The shadow's grip on Mary-Beth tightened, and she began to gasp, fighting for air, eyes rolling back in her head.

Greta was almost there, and she knew this would be the tricky part. Grabbing her friend, *and* holding onto the light. She did the best she could. She suddenly jumped the last few steps, wrapping one hand around Mary-Beth's outstretched leg, before turning tail and running once more.

It hurt, a lot. Mary-Beth was heavy, and she was slow. Mary's head hit each step as they went up, a horrible thud, thud, thud. She had to take a break every few steps, the weight of her body too much of Greta's frail hands. But the shadow was at her back. She could feel it now, its breath hot on her neck, one freezing cold hand on her shoulder, almost, almost close enough to...

But the salt it had thrown back towards her was working. She could feel the grit under her feet and she knew each step must be harder and harder for it. Finally, in what seemed more like petulant anger than an actual plan, it pushed her, sending her knees crashing into the next step. It hurt more than she could describe and she was sure she had broken something. But it had pushed her into the landing, into safety and out of darkness. She had left the door to the ground floor beautifully open, and life saving light was pooling out from it. She had to crawl the rest of the way, body too spent to do anything else. For a moment she just breathed, Mary-Beth's limp body next to her.

The ambulance came remarkably swiftly. She must have been in shock, or passed out, as she lost all sense of time from this point onwards. It seemed as if one moment she was calling the emergency line, and the next the ambulance was there, Mary-Beth being carried out on a stretcher.

Everyone assumed it was an accident, of course. An old lady falling down some stairs was hardly cause for a police investigation. And Greta was too scared to mention anything. If her best friend didn't believe her...who would?

They took her into hospital for the night, worried she had also hurt herself. With her leg throbbing fiercely, it certainly felt like she had. It hurt like hell, far worse than she thought it had any right too. But she didn't think too much of it. Instead, she begged the doctors for news of Mary-Beth, guilt and worry eating her alive. They wouldn't say much, as she wasn't an immediate family member, but they did say she was "stable, but critical."

She couldn't even imagine what injuries the poor woman must have. She tortured herself, endlessly trying to riddle it out. Did she have brain trauma, from her head hitting the stairs so much? Did her bones break when she fell?

And what had that thing actually done to her? What could cause your skin to go gray so quickly? Your eyes to look so manic, so horrible?

The one practical thing she did manage to do in hospital was to get someone to look after Delta. Davide happily agreed to take him in. He and his partner even bought a little cat bed.

"Well, at least that's something done," she muttered to herself, suddenly wishing she at least had Floppy with her. But of course, she didn't dare ask anyone to go into that house. By the time she had thought of it, the sun was starting to set. And what kind of fully grown adult wanted a stuffed toy anyway? No, she decided, she wouldn't hear of it, no matter how much good it would have done her.

She couldn't sleep at the hospital, of course. The doctors kept waking her up every ninety minutes, asking her stupid questions like "Do you know what year it is?" and "What's your name?" She knew they were trying to help, but she hated them, hated how they disturbed her brooding, hated how they could never possibly understand. She didn't want to go home, exactly. The very thought terrified her. She knew, logically, she should run far away, possibly even immigrate. There was a terror in her bones, lodged under her lungs. It made it hard to breathe somehow, her whole body unsteady and weak. And yet. She couldn't give up. She loved it too much. There was a wildness there, and a power that she just couldn't look away from. She wanted more, not less. And so, no matter how scared she was, how much she wanted to be sick, she headed home. No one would scare her away.

As always, driving up to the house was such a pleasure. She swore she had never seen a house finer than this one, and it was all hers. She felt a burst of proactiveness hum through her. It was beautiful, and it was hers, and that meant something. Even better, Davide was there waiting for her, Delta happily under his arm. Instantly, she felt relief burst through her chest. No matter how terrified she was, she was still so happy to see them.

"Oh, thank you," she said, rushing over to them.

"No worries at all! He's a delight. Welcome back anytime." Davide smiled. "I uh. He did manage to get out, I afraid. Bolted out the door and down to the seaside – we live very close, don't worry. Practically on the beach. I wasn't sure if that was okay...?"

"Oh," Greta said. She'd never actually thought about letting Delta out. It simply seemed that he had never wanted to, he spent the vast majority of his time sleeping or snuggling, which suited both of them fine. "Well, don't worry about it. I'm just glad he's safe."

She invited Davide in, but he didn't take her up on the offer. She was a little disappointed. But still, she took a deep breath and pushed the door open.

It struck her as strange that the house was exactly how she had left it. Surely, she thought, the ramifications of that event should have changed the house in some manner.

But it was all the same, side table she had so recently placed there still standing neatly in the corner, the rug still needing a vacuum. And the basement door still open.

She didn't want to go near it. She felt a sinking feeling in her gut just looking at it. But she also couldn't imagine it was a good idea to keep it open. She shuffled forward, wishing above all else that she could just have peace in her own house. She was just about to slam it shut when she saw it. A faint light tumbled down the stairs, illuminating the landing beneath.

The unopenable door was open.

She froze. Had Mary-Beth really had time to open it before the lights went out?

"Don't be ridiculous!" she said out loud. She could see that final moment clear as day. Greta hadn't even been able to let go of the keys before the darkness came. There was no way anyone had time to open the door, it just wasn't possible.

Finally, she believed. Not just in an abstract way, or a 'there are probably no other explanations' type of way. But she really accepted it, all of it. The ghosts, and hauntings, and all the strange noises, suddenly the reality of that seeped into her soul and her body, settling deep in her heart. Now she knew that this house was special, magical. That maybe, if she was both lucky and dedicated, she could have a slice of that magic. That she could do wonderful things.

She stood, still as the grave, almost all of her wanting to simply slam the door shut and run.

Almost all of her.

She had so many questions, such a deep need to know. A need that would make her risk everything, would inspire and torment her until she knew…everything. Was it bad that the door was open? Did it need to be shut again? Was it a trap? Why had she and her brother been able to spend hours down there, and Mary-Beth only moments? The door must be important, it must.

The truth was, she couldn't *not* look inside. It wasn't in her. She tried, backing away, making herself some toast in the kitchen. She even cleaned that rug, a job she particularly detested. She told herself a great many logical things: It was stupid to go down there again. It was probably a trap. The shadow was clearly intelligent, and almost certainly angry at her in particular. Even if she did investigate, the chances of finding anything useful were slim. It seemed a horrible way to die.

But the whole time, a question throbbed at the back of her mind.

What's down here?

It wasn't even a question she actively thought about, more of a pulse in her bones. It sat with her, the curiosity, the need to know.

What if there was a body down there, one that simply needed to be buried properly, a soul put to rest? What if it was a vampire that needed a stake through the heart? What if it was some horrifying monster that needed to be vanquished before it terrorized the whole world? More to the point, could she really live not knowing?

That question, at least, had a concrete answer. An answer she was wholly and completely confident in. No, she couldn't. She was going down.

Finally, she grabbed the salt, knowing that if she was going to do this it had to be now, before sundown, when at least she would have the rest of the house to retreat to.

She took every precaution she could think of. She bathed in salt, letting it run down her body as she showered. It was actually quite nice, it was an exfoliant after all. She pretended she was at some wonderful spa, pampering her body in preparation for some sinful night. She piled even more of it on her toast, although she hid it under a lovely layer of honey. She shoved handfuls of it in her pockets, spilling out and leaving a faint trail behind her everywhere she went.

And finally, she went down, taking the steps as quickly as she could manage after such a difficult few days. Salt still gritted the ground, a great comfort to her, and strangely she couldn't feel 'it' – that clammy coldness that he had now begun to associate with the shadow. Going down to the basement felt... normal. Still, she didn't linger.

She kept her eyes on the door, that flash of red which stood open like a bloody mouth. God, it was strange-looking, how did the color stay so vivid, after all these years? And why were there circles carved so neatly, so deliberately into it? She hated to think.

She gulped as she stepped over the threshold, holding her breath.

Nothing happened.

It was...nice. Dusty, to be sure, more filthy than the rest of the house combined. It seemed like no one had set foot inside for a hundred years.

It was filled with stuff. A closet stood open, crammed with silk and satin dresses. Greta pulled the skirt of one out and spread it in her hands. It was massive, and certainly ancient. Victorian, perhaps? She was no art historian and knew no more than that, but the long train and lace sleeves certainly suggested something old.

There were other things too. A traveling trunk, with the initials V. B. etched on it in flowery writing, the most beautiful pair of shoes she'd ever seen, an entire desk filled with porcelain figurines and a ladies' toilette, which even included a hairbrush complete with blonde gray stands. A diary.

A chill took over her. She flipped the book open, marveling at the neat, curved handwriting inside, glimpsing words here and there. She had to know what it said, feeling certain it contained some answers. But she didn't dare stay a moment longer. Grabbing the diary, she hustled upstairs, excitement overwhelming fear for just a moment as she contemplated what she held; answers.

She had a lot to think about. The day passed slowly, achingly so. She waited desperately for news of Mary-Beth, though none came. She busied herself cleaning, again, though there was less and less to do as time went on. She hated that. There was something so therapeutic about it. About the manual labor. About taking something bad and making it simply, undeniably better. She needed it more than she cared to admit. She found she was too worked up to read the diary, as each time she started her mind shot off in another direction, too excited to know what it said to pay attention. It was infuriating. No, she needed to rest and she knew it.

She went to bed early that night, glad to have Delta with her once more. She succeeded somewhat, forcing herself into a fitful sleep. But she woke up early the next day, her whole body singing with anticipation for the diary.

She rolled over, ready to start the day with vigor. Until she felt something squelch under her leg. She ripped the covers back, wondering what on earth it was. A leach, fat and bulbous with her blood, stared back at her. For a moment she was so revolted she couldn't do anything.

"Is this...yours?" She asked Delta, looking at him incredulously. "I know Davide said you'd got out, but my word. Where on earth would you pick up such a thing?" She picked it off her and marched to the bathroom, holding it out at arms' length, flushing it down the toilet with grim satisfaction. She'd have to get that cat looked at again, she decided, heading down to make herself breakfast.

She put the kettle on, Googling *Where do leeches come from?* as she did so. It was somewhat of a relief to find that while most were freshwater, some do come from the ocean. That must be it then. It was nice to know there was a mundane reason for this at least.

"Well, that must be it then," she said, giving the cat a good look-over for any other parasites. "I'm just glad you're okay." He mewed softly at her, nuzzling against her good leg. "Now," she said, "who wants to join me on the couch?" He followed her happily, leaping up onto the green velvet cushion and settling in for a long day's nap. She smiled down at him, overwhelmingly glad for such sweet company. But she knew she had work to do.

So, finally, she opened the book.

Chapter Six

July 5th, 1843

I think you should know that I am incredibly beautiful. I don't have to say this to most people, obviously, but as you are my diary, and therefore do not have eyes, I thought I should make it clear. It's not like you can see me, is it? Besides, it's important. I have porcelain skin, startling green eyes unlike any you've seen, and a cupid's bow mouth that curves into a devilish smile. So I'm told. My hair is long and golden blonde, with a perfect natural curve to it that is neither too much nor too little.

And of course, my figure is perfect, riding and exercising as I do every day. That's why this leg injury is such a bother. Mother says I 'simply must rest', but it's so intensely tedious. I fully plan to abandon you, dear diary, as soon as I can. I don't think I've ever sat with a book even this long, at least not willingly!

It's my own fault. In truth, I am too old to play such childish games. I am sixteen after all! But Henry, my brother, is always so persuasive. And he's older than I am! He should know better. But it was such a lovely day, with the breeze carrying in the scent of lilac and the sun kissing everything – my fair hair included – with this gentle, warm glow. How could you not be gay on a day like that?

Of course, we haven't strictly been allowed to play such rough games since we were children. But Sarah, the governess, had better things to be doing with the young ones. So, off we went. Running through the forest, my long skirts catching on mud and branches, but I didn't care. Sarah would deal with it. I was just about to catch my brother, the words "Tag, you're it!" already in my throat. And then – it was the strangest thing. I've been in those woods every day for most of my life. I know it almost better than my own house. I've never tripped before, never even stumbled. I know the woods. I don't understand why I fell over. But I did.

It almost felt like someone pushed me. I could have sworn I felt the pressure of a hand on my shoulder, breath, warm and sickly sweet on my cheek.

But of course that's insane. I would never admit that to anyone but you, dear diary. People would think me utterly mad, and I can't have that. Look, only a few moments in my hands and you are already a trusted companion! You're welcome.

Perhaps it's because of how badly I've been sleeping recently. The pain in my leg keeps me up, obviously. It's only a sprained ankle. Henry says I'm being a cry baby about it. To be honest, I agree with him, at least a little bit. It doesn't even compare to when my horse threw me and I fractured my arm, and I was fit as a fiddle then.

And it's not so much that it hurts – although it does, a little – it's that it's *worrisome*, in some strange way. I can't stop thinking about it. I keep tearing the covers back and looking at it, as if I expect something else to be there in its place. Why? I must just be going mad with lack of distraction.

But ah, yes. Sleep. It's hard to keep my eyes open most of the time, and yet I cannot fully sleep. It's maddening. I am so utterly exhausted, and yet pure, actual, unadulterated rest eludes me. The most comfortable thing I can do is simply lay back on the pillows, eyes closed, but ears pricked. I know I don't accidentally fall asleep because I can hear the comings and goings outside my room. I've been able to accurately report everyone's activities for the last two nights straight. Henry was most impressed and actually verified it. Anyway, I'm afraid I must go back to doing that again, my eyes are so heavy I can barely see the page.

Also, I should have mentioned this, but my name is Violet. Nice to meet you. I pray our acquaintance is short!

July 7th, 1843

I am still here, I have not abandoned you. Worry not. I think I was able to sleep last night because I had some awful dreams. I was lost in a maze and no matter what I did, I couldn't get out. It doesn't sound so terrifying when I put it like that, does it? No monsters or ghoulies to speak of. It just felt so long. And I felt so...hopeless. And that scares me. What if I get stuck like that? What if I end up somewhere I simply cannot get out of? What if I am simply stuck, never to experience anything but dull monotony? I can't imagine anything worse.

No sage advice? I don't know why I consult you at all, dear diary. Meredith would be a much better companion, but she's away in France. To be fair, she has written, and Georgina has been such a dear. William and Phillip both sent inquiries as to my health, a fact that we girls giggled over. I know they intend to court me soon. When it's appropriate, of course. I don't know who of the two I would pick. William is doubtlessly richer, but Phillip is the more handsome one. I think I shall find a man who is both.

Everyone had been so kind, apart from Henry, who I must say has been rather too much. He put leeches in my bed while I was sleeping.

STRANGE AND TWISTED THINGS

He denies it of course, but who else would it be? When I woke up, the fat, foul things were all over me. I do love him, but really. It's a bit juvenile. Phillip would never do such a thing!

My foot is the same. No better, no worse. Although my leg hair is coming in much thicker. Rather unladylike I must say!

July 10th, 1843

I'm sorry I haven't written in a while. There are some things that are difficult to say, even to you. Difficult to admit to myself, I suppose. But – and I know this is madness – I think there's something different about my foot. It seems to not entirely be mine. I mean, it is, obviously. It is attached to me, it follows my commands, I can feel it when I poke it with a pin (yes, I have checked). But it...there's something wrong with it. It feels foul, dirty almost. And the nails. They are growing in hard and cracked, larger than before, I'm sure, because the skin around it is red with its forced intrusion.

I must be going mad. I need to get out of this bed, and soon.

July 12th, 1843

I am not going mad.

July 13th, 1843

Henry put leeches in my bed again, and still, sleep comes in fits and starts.

July 15th, 1843

I have received an invitation to yet another ball, and I am determined not to miss this one! I have been replaying the dances in my mind. If I can't practice on my feet, I shall have to do so in my dreams! I shall not embarrass myself or my family. In truth I worry a little that Phillip may have forgotten me. He hasn't written in a few days, and I've been in this bed so long. Has he found somebody else? The doctors say that I can't have much longer left, although mother wants to be certain, of course. Can't have me with a limp, that would be unladylike, and then what would be the point of me?

They haven't actually come to look at me in quite some time though. The doctor is rather expensive, of course that isn't a concern for us, but – well. We have nicer things to spend it on.

July 16th, 1843

I am afraid. And I am disgusted. My leg is thickening, like a man's. At first it was just my foot, and its hideous, hideous nails, but now it is up to my knee, the skin on my leg hardened and weathered like a sailor's, the hair coming in thick and coarse. It just doesn't match the rest of me at all. I can't stop looking at it, I can't stop thinking about it. I swear it grows larger, and rougher and just *worse* with each passing moment.

I asked my mother to fetch my rosary. She thought me most strange! I haven't willingly engaged with that since...well. It's been a long time! I have to admit, I've never been a true fan of our Catholicism. It's most unfashionable here in England at the moment, I am sure it has held father back in his dealings. It's a miracle we have held onto as much wealth and land as we have, considering...well...all of history since Henry the Eighth! But still. It felt prudent to say a prayer or two, since...oh do i really have to say it? I deduced something horrible.

Something that you, oh wise and all knowing diary, probably figured out long before I did. I don't think the leeches are coming from Henry. Where they are coming from, I cannot say, but...I fear I must apologize to my brother.

I had the maid clean my entire room last night, including changing the sheets on the bed. I was even allowed to get up and sit by the window while she did it. When I rose from the chair, hobbling the short distance back to the bed with a cane, a leech fell from my skirts. Of course, I was horrified, screaming and yelling about Henry, insisting that the maids check my bed gown for more. They did, and found none.

Finally satisfied, I returned to bed, and...oh I hardly think I have to say it. Not five minutes later, I found more. But surely, surely they are not coming from me? I won't believe it. I won't. I have a plan. I will sneak down to the kitchens tomorrow, get some old cloth, tie it around my foot, making sure nothing can get in or out. After a full day, I shall check the cloth. I am confident I will find nothing.

July 17th, 1843

This is insanity! This is monstrous and unfair and I have done nothing to deserve this! I could barely make it half a day before the itching, and the discomfort and the *wriggling* got to me. I removed the cloth and could hardly see my skin through the hundreds of fat little bodies that clung to me, gorged on my blood, bulbous and shining in the low light of my candle.

There were so many that not all of them could find purchase, clinging to the fabric instead of my leg, falling into my bed as I unwrapped it. It was all I could do not to scream. I couldn't bear anyone else seeing this. Not yet. Hopefully not ever.

Have I offended God in some way? I don't understand. I am not a liar, I do not have lustful thoughts. I have never hurt anyone, much less killed them. I am vain, I'll admit. But I pray (sometimes. Well no less than my brother!), I go to church when I'm not on bedrest.

I do not believe that I deserve this. How – how could I? When I am a child that has barely ever left her father's estate? It would be a fitting punishment for vanity I suppose, but... I don't understand. And I'm not sure I can take this much longer.

I don't know what to do.

July 18th, 1843

I snuck out of my room last night. I went to father's study. I knew he had books there. I thought, perhaps maybe one would be of use? Did he also keep a diary perhaps, where he admits to angering some evil fairy? Or a long-forgotten history of the family, detailing some wrong we need to right for this curse to be lifted? Even a children's story with the merest, smallest hint of a clue would have been welcomed.

There was nothing.

And walking with that...thing attached to me was so very odd. It obeys me, as I said, although I do fear this may change one day. But it is so utterly different to the other leg that I walked with the strangest gait, one leg far heavier, and going far further than the other. There is no denying it. I am a monster.

July 16th, 1843
Later that day

Leeches everywhere. I can not handle this. I have to tell mother.

July 19th, 1843

It was awful, telling her. She screamed at me, asking what I had done. She even asked if I'd been with a boy, if that was the cause of this. Of course not! I've never so much as been alone with a man, except for Henry and my father. She didn't believe me at first, tutting about my childish tricks. But of course, I wouldn't have believed her, if our positions were reversed. I had to actually show her to make her believe. She turned white, staring at it for a long time. And then the yelling started. I thought she was going to hit me, she was so furious. On and on she went, screaming until her voice became hoarse. I just sat there. I didn't know what else to do.

The doctor came. He took one look at it and said an amputation was in order. An amputation! I actually fainted. Will I survive that? And even if I do – what will my life be like? I'll never be able to dance again. Or ride, walk, do anything normal people do. And of course the biggest question, the one I will never be able to escape, the one that haunts my dreams and fills me with dread...

Will anyone marry me?

I'm reminded of my dream. Being stuck. Nowhere to go, nothing to do. Is that my fate? To be some old, lonely, pathetic woman. No husband, no child. Useless. Was it a premonition of some kind? That would have seemed like a ludicrous idea only a few short weeks ago, but now... can I afford not to consider it? I want to run. My leg does work, hideous as it is. It would be easy to steal a horse, take the jewelry that clutters my writing desk, get food from the kitchens... and just go. Where to, I couldn't say. But at least I wouldn't be dead – a real risk considering what awaits me.

But what else can I do? If I do nothing, how much will it spread? Will it overtake my body completely? Will I become some sort of monster? I wish I had answers. I would do the right thing, if I knew what it was. But both options seem so horrid, and I don't have anyone I could ask. Can you imagine telling Georgina about this...thing? She'd laugh till she was sick. Or worse, be disgusted. Either way, she'd tell everyone.

Mother says that she will bring a priest tomorrow. I know I should be glad. Even if my body is no more, my soul will be at peace. But I can't help but be angry. What did I do to deserve this? Why me? I know. I know I sound like a petulant little child. But my future was supposed to be so good. So assured, so bright and glittering. They said, they all said, my mother, my father, my brother, my friends, my suitors...they all said I would be okay. And I believed them. Nothing else has ever seemed possible.

But the way mother looked at me... I fear that door has now been locked to me forever. I hate that fact more than anything.

My hand is shaking too much, I can't write more. The next time I write, I will either be a cripple, or an outlaw.

Chapter Seven

Greta put the book down and sighed. She was barely a few pages in and already her head was swimming.

Where were the leeches coming from?

At this, Greta's stomach rolled. She should have known Delta was too convenient of an excuse, too easy, too mundane. She leaned back in her chair, finding suddenly that it was hard to breathe. Her chest heaved in short, sharp gasps, trying to force more air into her lungs but somehow failing.

What was going on?

Was this diary-writer the girl Greta could hear crying at night? Her face creased into a frown. Should she have been...nicer? To the ghost?

She burst out into peals of laughter. Not because it was a particularly outlandish suggestion, but precisely because it didn't seem any more ludicrous than everything else she had been through recently. She decided to talk it through with Floppy, grabbing the stuffed owl and bringing him into the kitchen, hoping some chores would clear her mind.

"Well, it makes a certain sort of sense," she said, as she slowly did the dishes, the water warm and soothing against her skin. "I had always assumed it was just a trap, and thought no more about it. But if that was the case, wouldn't the ghost have given up eventually? It wasn't working and it was clearly intelligent." As always, she wished and wished Fredrick were there, the need for him hard and heavy on her heart. Instead, she focused on Floppy.

She looked at him, his plush little belly reminding her forcibly of Delta's. That poor cat, he wanted nothing more than a restful place to sleep and got a heartbroken old lady and a haunted house instead.

"And the room, the room with the curtains...The ones Davide bought over, you know? That room is still fine, has been ever since the curtains arrived. Despite the fact that I never salted it..." The plates clinked under her hands and the soapy water seemed delicately pretty as she gazed at it, words coming slowly from her.

"Was it possible that this girl, Violet, that she cared for it in some way? It was clear beautiful things were important to her," she wondered desperately. "But...her house was in England!" Forgetting the dishes, she looked around the room, as if the answer were to suddenly leap out at her. "This couldn't be the home she grew up in, surely? Not the one where...it happened. No, no, she said England. She said England specifically because of how much they disliked Catholics. So how...?"

She allowed herself to get lost in thought for a moment, bubbles twirling around her hands as she worked. It seemed as if she had so much more information, yet still not enough. It tormented her, this deep, aching need to know. The strange thing was, she didn't *want* to want to know. She wanted to be totally content, happy to do nothing but sit and knit like every other nice old lady. To bake cakes for the neighbors and simply accept what she couldn't change. She knew she'd be happier if she just let go.

But that just wasn't interesting. It wasn't enough, it wasn't exciting at all. And how she missed excitement, missed daring and risk. Obsession consumed her, dragging her forward onto a path she knew was dangerous. It felt like she was a marionette on a string, this drive much more a need than a want. She was powerless to it, trying to keep up with it, to sate a greedy beast inside her that demanded answers. She knew it would never let her rest, not until she had satisfied it.

It was exhausting. She tried to take a break from it, tried to excuse herself for just a moment by gazing at the soap bubbles again, hoping that their familiar beauty would distract her. She certainly had enough to be getting on with, she reminded herself firmly, without reading the mad ramblings of a Victorian child. She had promised herself she would go to the hospital today to check on Mary-Beth. Her stomach churned at the thought of it. Not just of how her friend might look, might be feeling, but the part she now knew she had played.

"I can't believe I let her stay," she said, too ashamed to look Floppy in the eye. "You know, I think…I think I had hoped that the diary would have some answer for her. A cure. One thing that would make us both leap up and say 'Oh! Of course, it's so simple.' Something that would make it all better."

She wiped angrily at her face, trying to stop the flow of tears. It didn't help of course. Her hands were wet, so her face become even more so. But at least she could pretend crying wasn't the reason.

She hated herself for what happened that day, for not insisting more. She knew she had been right, knew she wasn't crazy. It's just that Mary-Beth had made it all seem so reasonable, as if a normal explanation wasn't only likely, but so obvious it was mad of her not to see it. She had made her feel stupid for even suggesting such a thing.

So it was with a heavy heart that she got in her car, bringing a bag of sweets just in case. She doubted Mary-Beth would be able to eat them, wasn't even sure if she was awake or not. But it seemed wrong not to bring anything at all.

Driving to the hospital was a far longer journey than she had remembered. She had probably been in shock before. She was glad she didn't remember much of it, she hated driving on those rural paths, so narrow and winding. More than once she had to brake suddenly as another car shot past her, far too close for comfort. By the time she arrived she was profoundly stressed, nerves on edge and shoulders tight.

Eventually she made it, the tall imposing building looming before her as she pulled into a parking space. They had tried to make the hospital nice, with colorful balloons and children's artwork. It did nothing to lighten the mood, Greta noted, only made it seem sinister and forced, as if you weren't 'allowed' to be sad here.

Her mood worsened when she arrived at reception and was told that she wasn't allowed to see her friend, due to not being family. She dithered for a moment, unsure of what to do. She couldn't imagine arguing, she wasn't that kind of person. But. Well. She was simply at a loss, unmoored and alone.

Thankfully, it was at that moment a voice rang out. For a moment, she thought it was Mary Beth, they seemed so similar.

"Greta! Hello!"

She squinted in confusion at the tall, thirty-something woman who was gazing at her expectantly, before it came to her. Francesca. Mary-Beth's niece. She had only met her once, and was not in the mood to exchange niceties.

"Hello...dear," Greta said through gritted teeth. "How are you?"

The girl – well, woman; anyone under the age of fifty looked girlish to Greta – launched into quite a long story about herself, her kids and how difficult it was for them all to have Mary-Beth in the hospital. Greta couldn't bring herself to care in the slightest. She was just tired, she told herself, very, very tired.

STRANGE AND TWISTED THINGS

"How is she?" she finally asked, when the time seemed appropriate.

She'd had a stroke they said, at just the wrong moment, making her fall down the stairs. The fall itself must have caused trauma, and she may have even had an aneurysm at the same time.

"I can't believe how someone could get so unlucky. All that at once!" the niece said. "I'm sorry you can't go in, but I'm not sure you want to. She's in horrible shape."

"Of course, I understand. Has she...said anything?" She asked, nervous for some reason she couldn't understand. Even if Mary-Beth told her family everything, which Greta knew she wouldn't, no one on earth would believe an old lady with a head injury. Even if they did, Greta hadn't done anything wrong. She felt slightly uneasy nonetheless, just the smallest seed of guilt wrapping around her spine.

"I'm afraid not." Francesca said, sighing. "We're hoping she's just too out of it on pain meds. But...it's possible there has been permanent damage. It's just too early to say."

She murmured her concern, and only a few minutes after she arrived, she left again, heading home with a lump in her throat. So she was not in the best of moods when her brother's name popped up on her phone. He had tried to call her yesterday as well, but she'd ignored it. With a groan she jabbed the accept button, letting his voice jump out at her from the car's speakers.

"What's this I hear about Mary-Beth?" he demanded, not even bothering to say hello. Mark and Mary had never been close friends, but they were certainly aware of each other. There was no way to avoid that really, with your sister's closest companion. She had been at their house so much when they were children, she practically lived there.

"Oh," she said, taking a deep breath. "She...well. She's stable, so that's something."

"What happened?" he demanded. She couldn't tell if he was worried or angry.

"She fell," Greta replied, with a finality that shocked her. It wasn't the full truth. But it was the only possible thing she could say to her brother and the lie came easily to her lips. "We were going into the basement. She was going to help me clean a bit – you know, *as friends do.*" She was surprised at the bitterness that had crept into her voice. But she meant it. Mary-Beth would never have dreamed of asking her for money, she could be appalled at the very idea. Still, she didn't pause long enough for him to react. "And, well. I'm not sure what happened. She must have misplaced her footing or something, because the next thing I know...she had collapsed."

Mark tutted. "I knew that house was too big for you." He said, voice full of righteous indignation. "I *told* you."

"Well, I wasn't the one that fell," she said tartly. It sounded horrible to her ears, but it was true. And she was tired of being told what was too much for her – they had no idea what she faced every day. They wouldn't believe her even if she told.

"You need to sell," he declared, "I'll get in touch with a realtor."

"What?" she screeched, accidentally jamming on the brakes for just a second. Luckily no one else was driving near her. "You have no right to do that," she said, a little calmer now.

"I can put you in a home," he stated, as if it wasn't her worst nightmare.

"No, you cannot," she countered. She knew a lot about this, it had been one of the many obsessions that had kept her up late at night. "You would have to obtain legal guardianship over me, and to do that you'd have to go to court. Even if you could be bothered to do such a thing, you wouldn't win. So please stop trying to bully me."

There was a long silence.

"I'm just worried about you," he said finally. "Besides, it's a huge house. Frederick gave it to you. You could sell it now and make a fortune!"

"I'm not selling the last gift Frederick gave me," she said with finality. She was proud that her voice didn't crack the way it usually did when she said his name. "And I'm not going over this again. Look, I appreciate your concern, but that's really all there is to it."

Her brother sighed. "Well, I just wish you'd think of the next generation, That's all."

"What?" she asked, having no idea what he was talking about. "I don't have any children, you know that."

"No but you have a nephew!" He shot back, clearly affronted that she hadn't thought of him.

"Oh. Right." She said, suddenly embarrassed. She liked Nicco well enough, but she hadn't seen him in years. He called on birthdays and Christmases, but it was clear to everyone it was a duty rather than a joy, and frankly it was one she could do without. Besides, she wasn't a huge fan of how he lived.

"You know he isn't doing too well. The money would mean a lot to him at the moment," he said, clearly trying to keep his voice even.

"Now?" She said, so shocked she almost drove off the road. She had thought he meant in her will or something- an issue she still had not come to a conclusion on.

"Yes, now! The boy needs money."

"He's not a boy," she shot back. "He is twenty-four years old. And I still don't know what happened to the last lot of money I gave him, I assume it was gambled," she sniffed, fully aware of the predilection that seemed to run rampant in that side of the family.

"How dare you," Mark hissed. Greta just rolled her eyes. "That boy is honest, hard-working, respectful – "

"He is greedy, entitled and nasty." She snapped before she could stop herself. Well, it was true. Frederick had hated him, hated how he was only interested if you had something he wanted, how he assumed if he needed something he was owed it. Greta couldn't help but agree. Why hadn't *he* come to help her get settled in? He was young and healthy, didn't he care about his aging old aunt? Clearly not. Selfishness, that was the only reason she could think of. Or apathy. She didn't know which was worse.

"That's my son you're talking about," he bellowed.

"Well then, he's your responsibility," she said tartly, lips pursed.

And then he said the words she knew he would say. The words he had been saying to her since they were children "If you don't do as I say, you'll regret it." She just hung up the phone.

She didn't understand why she wasn't loved. She was good at it, she felt, good at giving affection. She enjoyed making other people happy, was more than ready to go far out of her way for them. She found people truly fascinating, genuinely wanted to know all their concerns, their hopes, their joys. The mundane details other people found dull, she found electric. It was a pleasure to understand people. And love... love was such an active joy. A gift to give over and over again, an action that bought her close to rapture. She wanted to love, more than anything else in the world.

But she had never really found anyone to do the same for her. She thought she had, in Frederick. She mused on him as she drove, thinking back to their earliest days, their best vacations. Even last Christmas she had been blissfully happy, having no idea Frederick was anything but overjoyed with the life they had built together.

She allowed her mind to wander, talking to her ex-husband in her own head like an imaginary friend.

So when his name popped up on her phone, for just one moment she assumed she was imaging it. It took a few seconds to sink in, the fact that this was, actually, really real. She pulled to the side of the road, shaking. Her heart was racing far harder than it ever had in her haunted house, her breath coming in waves of panic. She didn't know what to do, couldn't imagine ignoring him, but if she reacted this way just to seeing his name, what would it be like to hear his voice? She honestly worried she'd pass out.

But of course, she couldn't *not* pick up the phone. Couldn't ignore it. She had to know.

She forced herself to focus, feeling the steering wheel beneath her hands, the clothes on her back. She gave herself time for her breathing to level, closing her eyes and thinking of anything she could to calm down. Oh, how she wanted to let go of him, how she wanted him not to matter. But she couldn't, it just wasn't in her nature. He did matter. He meant the world to her. With a long, slow sigh, she picked up the phone.

"Greta," he said in that deep, smooth voice she knew so well. And the tears came, just as she knew they would. But she fought to keep her voice steady, breathing deeply, forcing herself to focus.

"Sorry I took a while to pick up. I almost missed the phone!" She tried to force out a laugh. "What can I do for you?" She had very deliberately avoided the phrase 'Sorry I missed you.' It was too close to the truth, too close to admitting that she missed him every single day. It would have made her break down completely. And her pride was too strong to allow for that.

"Oh yes. Of course. So, uh, how have you been?" he said. God, it was so unnatural to talk to him like this. Like strangers that had only met a handful of times. She wanted to tell him everything, spew her guts out before him. To really have him understand. Instead, she chose her words carefully.

"Okay," She lied. "You?"

"Yes," He said. And then there was silence. She couldn't take it, not with him.

"So do you think you made the right choice then?" she blurted out, trying and failing to sound casual. But she had to ask him. Had to know. Fuck her pride, she decided wildly, though she knew she would regret it later. Nothing was more important than this.

Instead there was a long, long pause.

"Mark says you haven't been doing so well. There was a fall?"

This threw her completely. Torn between pursuing her line of questioning and raging about why her brother was contacting her ex-husband, her only reply was to splutter wordlessly.

"I worry about you in that house," he continued, not unkindly. "I should have known it was too big for you to handle on your own, I just didn't... I didn't want to take that away from you as well, I suppose."

She didn't reply. She didn't think she could without bursting into tears.

"Listen, Greta," he said, his voice so familiar it made her want to keen. Instead, she rocked back and forth in her seat, as if her emotions simply had to burst out of her through motion if not sound. At least this way was silent and Frederick didn't have to know. "I think you should sell it. I – I worry about you. The last thing I want is for you to be hurt. I still care..." Here, he let out a long breath. "Your brother. Mark. He said...he said it was something of a labor of love of yours. Some kind of grand gesture, almost ro –"

No.

No, for some reason, that was too much.

She pulled the phone away from her face, furiously jamming the red button, throwing it into the back seat, not caring if it cracked. She couldn't face it, couldn't handle it, couldn't take that voice, that beautiful, wonderful voice that she had known for so long, sounding so cold, so empty. So far away.

She loved him. She loved him with a power that resonated through her whole body, that made her chest ache and her throat sting.

Her body shook with it.

"How could he? How could he?" she screamed, not sure if she meant her brother or Frederick. Yes, her home, the whole house was a labor of love. It had all been for him, every wall she scrubbed, every floor she cleaned had been an expression of how much she loved him. Every single one of them. She had wanted to build a monument to him, something grand and lasting that would radiate her love like a beacon. Her love was big enough for that. It demanded space, glory, attention.

But it felt ugly, suddenly, allowing people to gawp at it. It was for him, but somehow., she suddenly realized, it wasn't for him at all. It was a reflection of her, of her stubbornness, and hope, and tenacity. She had enriched the house, not him. She had done all the work, lifted it up from a ruin into a real home. It was a testament to her power to endure and create. Like an artist picking up a brush and depicting the finest sunset, one did not compliment the sun on the beauty of the painting. No, that was the work of the painter, everyone knew that. So it was with her, she suddenly felt. Her subject was...undeniably exquisite. But she was the artist.

Not knowing what else to do, she raced home, threw herself back on her bed, and opened the diary once more. Perhaps Violet would have something to say about it.

Chapter Eight

July 20th, 1843

Well. I did it. Henry and father held me down. The doctor suggested his colleagues do that part, but mother didn't want strange men around me. I would like to think that this was some bizarre impulse to protect my modesty, but I have a feeling it was to keep our secret close. Either way, I'm glad.

It hurt more than I can possibly tell you. They gave me brandy, so much that I almost passed out, but it didn't help. I can still see the scalpel as they approached me, the light glinting off of it. I was surprised how small it was. I mean it wasn't tiny but it didn't seem enough, it didn't seem...real, somehow. Not until it cut into my flesh. Then it became everything. They cut through the skin, just above my knee, where it was still soft and smooth like a lamb. That stung. Worse than anything I had ever experienced up to that point.

The next knife was bigger, closer to the butcher's cleaver I had imagined, although somehow much worse, bigger, badder. It looked mean, somehow, still bloody from the last time they used it. I couldn't help but wonder for a moment if the last person to have that knife inflicted on them had lived or died. And then I found I didn't care. I couldn't, the pain was too extreme for any rational thought, as it hacked into my muscle, blood pooling on the table as I screamed. Next, the bone saw. It was torture, pure and simple.

The table shook as they worked it into me, back and forth. I prayed that I would pass out from the pain, shocked that I hadn't. But still, unconsciousness somehow refused me.

I felt the bone finally snap, giving way to the saw. The rest of my leg they half cut, half ripped from me. I don't want to speak of it any more.

I pray that it was worth it. I fear that it was not.

July 21st, 1843

Henry has been kind. I haven't apologized about accusing him of putting leeches in my bed, and he has not brought it up again. He knows my pride can't take admitting I was wrong. Not right now. But, to my absolute delight, I have not seen the nasty things again. Three days since the amputation and not a single one! Gosh how lovely that thought is. How truly divine. Please, for my sake, take a moment and celebrate the fact that around you right now- *there are no leaches!!!* What a simple joy! Perhaps the amputation worked. Perhaps the blessing from the priest did. I don't care. It's over and that is all that matters.

I'm going to eat more chocolate.

July 22nd, 1843

Well. Phillip has officially moved on from me. No surprise there. Everyone has heard about my convalescence now. (Mother spun some story about how the leg was much worse than we thought. Not just a sprained ankle, but a break in fact. Tragic, but understandable. If you ask me, a doctor would have to be blind to confuse the two, and anyone hearing that tall tale would have to be almost comically stupid to believe it, but there you go. It's the story and we are sticking to it).

He sent me a letter addressing me as "sister" and wishing me well, but mentioning how much fun the last ball was. And we all know he couldn't take his eyes off of Lady Pertemers' daughter. I expect the same from William soon.

July 25th, 1843

Sorry I haven't written in some time. Henry has been taking me outside! When there is no one around to see, of course. Oh it's marvelous. It's strange now, to see the forest. I can't help but feel… a little hurt. As if I somehow expect it to apologize. Another mad whim, I know. It won't actually happen, even I am not crazy enough to think it will. But still. It's how I feel.

It's funny, I never really thought of that day since it happened. I was too consumed with the…issues, I suppose. But with all that has happened…. Did I really fall? Or was I pushed? I re-read what I wrote in here, about feeling someone touch me. I can't quite believe it. Still, after all this, it seems too fantastical to contemplate. But…well, surely it's no more strange than the other things that have been going on of late? I'm sorry, I know I sound mad. Ignore me. I don't even know what I'm suggesting…A ghost? A poltergeist?

A demon?

I hope not. I feel as if even writing that word invites it somehow. And surely the priest would have said, if he had felt something of the devil. And he would know. He's the expert. I don't know why I am expected to deal with this, why God (or, heaven forbid, The Devil) put this in front of me. I just have to trust that everyone else knows what they are doing. The priest, the doctor, mother.... Surely, one of them would know if it was truly evil? Someone would notice.

July 26th, 1843

I wish I could lock all this away. Put it behind a door, hide it, like they hide me. Somewhere fortified, where only the bravest can go. Where these strange and twisted things can't hurt anyone at all. Well, unless they deserve it. I truly don't believe that I did. I don't know who would, to be frank, but I suppose that is not for me to decide. It is for God, if he still listens, or indeed, if he exists at all.

July 28th, 1843

How foolish I was to think I'd move on from you "when this is all over". I'm not sure if there is anyone apart from you and Henry left. Mother won't look at me. I know she hasn't told father the whole truth, because he still visits me everyday, hugging and kissing me, asking after my health. I can't imagine how he'd react if he found out. Certainly not like this.

I've been looking at my gowns, you know. And my hats. There's one dress I adore in particular, made of baby blue silk, with a low neckline and short sleeves trimmed with lace, white stain bustled in the back to make a long train. Ah, how good I looked in it! It made my eyes sparkle and dance, and my waist...ah! I wish you could have seen it. Everyone agreed how good I looked, even Beatrice, who famously hates me. And then I have a dinner dress of lilac and green, princess cut, embroidery everywhere. I didn't wear that one enough. In truth it was not particularly flattering around the bust, but it is exquisitely made. I looked elegant in it, stately. Like a real woman, and not some girl. I should have worn it more. It's not that I can't wear them again, it's that it is different now. No finery will ever erase the fact that I am damaged, that I fell and God did not save me, not entirely. I am not whole.

I imagine that I will still marry, and so that is a blessing. Some old man will get a bargain out of me, a younger, prettier, richer woman than he could have dreamt of otherwise. He will get his money's worth, and I will not be a disgrace. So that is something, at least I will still be able to hold my head up high.

There is one question that has been weighing heavily on my mind, I'm almost too afraid to ask, but I suppose I can start with you. You at least will not judge me... Can I still have children? I do wish you could tell me.

I've wondered about that a lot recently. Mother asked if I had given myself to a man, if that was the cause of... all this. So presumably, there is some connection? She would know, she is married after all. I hadn't of course, I would never do that before marriage. But I had thought about it, a little. And I did read Phillips letters an awful lot. Is that enough...? They say sinful thoughts have power. I wish I could ask Mother. But she only comes to see me when Henry drags her here, and god knows I can't ask in front of him.

I have never been close to my mother. But I suddenly feel as if she is locked away from me now, as if something between us has been forever shut away. She knows that deep down, I am ugly. And I think she hates me for it.

August 12th, 1843

I'm sorry I have not written in some time. Everything just feels so hopeless, so boring and dull that not even my diary should be saddled with the monotony.

I have been given a wheelchair, and that is some comfort. It's nice to be able to move around as I wish. I have decided that I am going to go to a ball next week. It won't be the same, obviously. But, I think it will be good to show people that my face has not been damaged, that I still have my fire and spirit. Oh well, I suppose that's really the only thing I have to say. I'm sorry I'm so dull. I'll tell you how it goes.

August 20th, 1843

Well. That was a disaster. It made me wish I was really a witch, so I could curse them all. It hurt more than I can tell you, to have to sit to the side and simply watch as the others danced. People were…kind. Well, polite, I guess you would say. They inquired after my health and smiled as I told them I was recovering. The chaperones made sure I had company.

I sat with the ugly girls, watching even as they danced occasionally. They were nicer than they had to be, I'm big enough to admit that. There is a hierarchy to the way these things go, to how the women act. And I was always very confident in my position. I can't say I was ever kind to them. I wasn't horrible, of course, not mean, not rude, but… Oh, I think you know what I mean, I don't think I have to say it. I'm sorry for that, and I'm doubly sorry that now it's too late to do anything about it. Oh well, it's over now. They were gracious to me and I respect them for that.

It's just the way people spoke to me, as if I had lost my wits as well as my leg, their words overly enunciated, careful to not use any long words. Ug, how I hate it. I was hardly a bookworm (oh, that has changed by the way, I am now an avid reader) but I was always lively. That hasn't changed. I can't bear the pity in their eyes, the way they clearly pat themselves on the back for even having a conversation with me, their good deed for the day done. And how they congratulate me for the simplest of things! I wheeled myself over to the window at one point and you would have thought Jesus had turned water into wine once more, the way they reacted!

God I hated it. And to think how much I used to enjoy those things.

That was perhaps the worst bit. I know, I *know* that if it wasn't for this awful leg I would have been the belle of the ball. I always used to be.

And yes, yes, I'm getting over it, getting used to it. Thanking God for my life and counting my blessings and all that. It just hurts. It hurts to see everything I could have had, but for some tragedy I don't understand. It hurts, physically, a weight in my chest and my stomach. And I don't know what to do about it.

August 26th, 1846

Mother forced me to another ball. It's as if, now I've finally broken the seal, entered into the public eye once more, she sees me as being real again. She actually helped me pick my dress this time, taking care to select one that draped well over my chair. And that showed off my bosom, of course.

I did actually, surprisingly, meet someone quite nice there. He spoke to me as if I wasn't a child, his smile was wide and arms were strong and inviting. I wanted to touch them, though I dared not. I still don't know if my...affliction is contagious, and if it can be spread through...well...that.

He, of course, has no money. He's the third son of a Baron well-known to be riddled with debt, I never would have looked at him before. But he was kind. And, truth be told, he was handsome.

It had never occurred to me that I might marry for love. Of course, it's all the rage these days isn't it. I mean, our Queen is so clearly besotted with Prince Albert, it would be mad if the rest of us didn't try and emulate that. But, I don't know. I've never had feelings like that for a member of the opposite sex before. I mean, I haven't met many of them. So I just don't know…what to expect, I suppose. I do know about wealth and power and titles. So I suppose that is what I always dreamed of. Do I dare dream of anything else?

September 1st, 1846

I did not dream of that, and now I am glad. Another ball come and gone, and a far more 'suitable' suitor has been found.

He is twice my age, with a sour expression and no talent for conversation. I would be his third wife, the other two dying in childbirth. From the way he looked at me, I could guess he wouldn't mind the same fate for me, if it meant the same pleasures for him.

He has a title (and the debts to go with it), and a large estate near Wales. Mother is happy. Well, relieved would probably be a better word. She keeps saying "Well. That's settled then." It's become like a mantra to her. I can tell father is a little disappointed, he wanted better for me. But he has been an acquaintance of the man for some time and claims him to be "an agreeable sort of fellow, once you get to know him."

As for me…I don't know. It's probably better than I could reasonably expect, given the circumstances. I was terrified that I wasn't going to get an offer at all, you know. Simply be left as a spinster, all alone somewhere, the mad old lady they keep hidden away. At least I have avoided that fate.

And now, we shall have a few more brief conversations, meetings in public places – typically we would walk together, but clearly... that is no option. And then we shall become engaged. I suppose mother will make us wait at least six months, lest it looks like the wedding was too rushed. God she would hate another scandal like that, especially if I do fall pregnant soon after the wedding. How people would talk, that I threw myself at some old man! But it is effectively all decided. He is to be my husband.

September 10th, 1846

I find I can tolerate him less and less with each meeting. God knows how bad it will be when we are married. I can't even begin to describe to you how insufferable he is. It is not one thing, not one huge, unavoidable issue (though of course his age, lack of wit and stubborn temper should be enough). It is <u>everything</u>. Every small, tiny thing he does drives me utterly mad! From the way he smacks his lips without saying anything to the one-word responses he gives me when I try to speak, to how he smells (like horses), to how he looks at me (vulgarly). No, I'm sorry, I cannot bear to think of him for one more second.

September 17th, 1846

I don't know what I do with my days, you know. I sleep somewhat better than when ...the ugliness was attached to me, but still, I toss and turn each night, so much that I'm exhausted by the morning. And the days seem to just...drift by. I draw. I practice my French. But I find that I have nothing to write because I do so little. How often I have opened this book, but simply hovered my hand above the page, having nothing to report. I am boring and I cannot stand it. You deserve a more interesting companion than I.

November 1st, 1846

The date of the wedding has been set. April 11th, 1847. If you squint at it, it looks rather like April Fools day. Oh how I wish it was just a joke.

January 26th, 1847

It is my birthday. So very different from other years. At least then, people pretended to care.

February 1st, 1847

I've started to struggle to sleep again. In *that* way, if you understand me. The ugly way. It crept up on me gradually. Until one morning I realized, I don't think I've actually slept for days. Ever since that realization, I've been randomly bursting into tears. I tell people it's because I'm sad to leave my family. That makes father smile, at least.

I try to smile back, but every day there is a pit at the bottom of my stomach, and I know it will never leave me. Sometimes I wonder if I should just make peace with it, just accept it daintily. Ladies are supposed to do that, are they not? Of course, all are supposed to fight against the devil, Father Michaels is quite clear about that. But... I honestly don't know how they expect me to. I will try, I will. I just fear I am already doomed.

February 10th, 1847

Still no leeches, I check every morning.

February 22nd, 1847

No leeches, thank god, although every pain I have in my other leg causes me such deep worry I want to be sick. I check it constantly. Nothing to report yet, thank the good Lord. (I pray every day now). Please, if you can, whoever may find this, or read this or steal a page – pray for me too. I am very afraid.

March 27th, 1847

I want to start writing again, dear diary. I do feel that you are the only friend who has not abandoned me. I just find this heaviness upon me. And I don't want to simply complain, it only makes things worse I find.

Instead I shall tell you about the wedding. It is all moving ahead rather well, and I find that I actually am becoming excited about some aspects. My dress, of course. Don't laugh, I can hear you, you know! I know it's rather vain of me, but...I just can't help it! Father treated me to a new one, a rare treat and possibly an extravagance for a disabled daughter soon to leave for her husband's home. But it's beautiful. All white, as is the new trend (just like the Queen!), with flowing lace and embroidered roses in silver cascading down the bodice. I keep looking at it, asking the maids to pull it out and drape it across the bed for me. I can almost dream again. I want to hold it tight, to bury my face in it. To never let go.

And I am being allowed to choose the flowers. I want hydrangeas, I think, and wild rose. The flowers will be beautiful, even if I am not.

I think I value beauty, because in many ways it is peace. It shuts out the ills of the world, it demands you forget everything else, everything you're afraid of or ashamed about. You simply admire it. For that single second, where it commands your attention and holds your heart, it is everything. All else falls away. It reminds you that some things simply have value, not for what they can do or who they know, but purely for what they are.

It can take your breath away with reverence for the moment, with adoration for what is standing before you.

And I think that has meaning. I think that's important. Not silly or childish or vain. I'm so utterly sick of apologizing for being vain. I lost something very valuable to me. My beauty was my world, my life. And I am furious that it is gone.

Chapter Nine

Greta woke up the next morning with the diary open on her chest. She hadn't wanted to put it down, hoping the girl would say something actually relevant to the situation. But as the pages flew past, she felt that she couldn't stop herself from pitying Violet.

What if that was the thudding sound she heard on the stairs? The poor girl's wooden leg, surely she was going to get one of those eventually?

It still didn't make any sense, because the girl was clearly from England, not Italy, but... well, surely it was possible? Their ailments were so similar, there had to be a connection. To think otherwise wasn't just straining the limits of credulity, it was laughably moronic. No, she was willing to believe in ghosts and ghoulies, but not bald-faced, random chance. That would just be stupid, she decided, willful ignorance.

And the crying too, what if that was her on her wedding night? What if the ghost was simply sad?

She closed her eyes, sighing. She wanted that to be the case so badly. As if her pure love could come in and fix everything, her strength of empathy enough to vanquish all.

She doubted it.

But...what if she were to find out? Her experimentation had stopped with the salt, clinging to the flimsy protection it offered. But surely that wasn't it, wasn't the only way to dance with the energies in this house. She bit her lip, thinking hard. The curtains, the original ones, they were still untouched, despite the fact that she had not "protected" them with her salt wash. Was that good, or bad? Did it mean the demon was happy there, content to do nothing, or unable, trapped somehow in the folds of history. Well, she decided, standing slowly, her joints popping, stability was good. Harmony. Tranquility. Peace. It would have to be enough.

She headed back down to the basement, where she was unsurprised to see the mysterious door already hanging open, despite her deliberate choice to close it the last time she was down here. Strangely, it brought a smile to her lips this time, something about the predictable nature of it comforting, as if she were beginning to know the house, a little like a friend. As quickly as she could, she gathered some things – an ancient violin, a perfume bottle now empty, the silver mirror and hairbrush set.

She didn't dare take more, fearing she had lingered too long already.

For the first time, she was excited for night to come. She had carefully laid out her new belongings in the drawing room, the only room that now stood unsalted. The violin leant next to the door, the hairbrush and mirror on the side table, the perfume bottle next to it.

Would the demon like it, or not? She wondered as the sun set, her room filled with an almost golden glow.

"If my theory is right, at least one of those items will have moved by the time I go downstairs, this is just a young girl that wants her baubles." She told Floppy as she climbed into bed, Delta curled happily at her feet. It was lovely, actually, by far the calmest she had been since…well, she couldn't remember when, actually. For the first time in a long time, she was actually looking forward to the next day.

But she didn't have to wait that long. That night, instead of crying, the most incredible violin music filled the air, a tune sweet and romantic. Haunting, yes, in the way that only strings can be. But so exquisitely beautiful.

Her face cracked into a smile.

She wouldn't be able to tell you exactly why she found this significantly less threatening than the crying, but she did. Perhaps because she had some power over it, some agency to choose which one she preferred to hear. Perhaps because she had a sense that somehow, her choices had made someone happy. Either way, she was less afraid that night. Not quite happy but, at the very least, at peace.

She didn't sleep, but at this point she didn't truly expect to. Not with what Violet had said in her diary, not with how thoroughly rest had eluded them both. She accepted it mildly, adapting quickly to this new truth, almost enjoying it. At least she didn't feel so alone any more, didn't lie awake, night after night, eyes closed, wondering what she was doing wrong. At least she knew it wasn't her fault. It was nice to let go of that particular struggle. Sleeping had always been hard without Fredrick and it was almost a badge of honor to realize that now, she would never, ever sleep well without him. It seemed fitting, somehow.

She sighed, knowing she would never be able to convince a doctor to amputate her leg, or have the stomach to do it herself. It seemed that she was simply stuck with it. She idly looked down, picking leeches off her skin and flicking them into the bin next to the bed. This too, she had got used to.

In some strange way, it wasn't as bad as she thought it would be. Proof, real proof that the afterlife existed was actually profoundly calming. It seemed to be a dark and chaotic place for sure, but then wasn't this life? It seemed better to her than just falling into a void, becoming nothing.

She looked down at her ankle, a faint smiling curling her lip. In truth, she hadn't noticed 'the ugliness' as Violet had put it. Her legs were already time worn, thick and pock marked. But now that she was looking for it, she could see it. The toenails were certainly larger, dirtier than they had any right to be, and the hair was certainly thicker than it had ever been before. It was rather hideous. Whatever, she reasoned, no one was likely to see her legs anyway.

The next morning she was up as soon as light had filled the room, impatiently waiting for when she felt it was safe to leave. She had a plan. Once more she emptied the nearby stores of salt, even traveling into Florence to raid their megamarts. It was a big job, and took most of the day. She kept having to explain to people why she needed so much, kept pressing them to check the back, just to be sure. People couldn't help but wonder, staring openly at her, eyebrows raised. She found she didn't care. They were wrong, all of them. They didn't understand, only she did. She found she liked having secrets like that, it made her feel powerful, and wise. She hadn't felt like that in some time.

Finally, after her sixth store, she came home, laden down with her treasure. Almost reverently, she sprinkled an aisle, each side fat and tall, leading from her bedroom to the drawing room, ending in a neat little dead end. She didn't want to invite anything back after all.

She had noticed a pattern, over these long nights. The crying (or the music) always began between eleven o'clock and eleven forty-five. Tonight, she wanted to see. Perhaps she was being reckless, finally tuning into that silly old woman she had always feared becoming. But she wanted to know, so badly. It seemed worth the risk.

And so, at exactly eleven o'clock that night, she was standing in her cage of salt, looking out across the living room. Nothing happened. The violin leaned against the wall, lifeless and still. She felt ridiculous. It suddenly occurred to her – why don't the ghosts just fly over the salt? Is that not possible? Or even just step over it? If they can't, how high up does this mysterious power go? Surely not all the way to space, or she wouldn't have had to do every single room in the house, only the first floor would have been necessary. But to the ceiling at least, because otherwise –

And here her musings ended.

Violet, if indeed that is who she was, was truly as beautiful as she had claimed. She hadn't done herself justice, in fact. There was elegance in the way she moved, the way her hips swung gently from side to side, the way her cheeks caught the light. She was so breathtaking, it was impossible to look away. And then the violin began to play. A man suddenly appeared next to her, dressed head to toe in green and gold. His face was almost as stunning as her's, fresh and youthful, with dark eyes full of lust and luscious black hair. He was lithe too, his body slim but strong, graceful and poised.

He grabbed her hand and they began to dance, twirling around each other with unimaginably fluid movements. Greta couldn't help but gasp, skin suddenly tingling with admiration. It was sublime, beyond anything she had witnessed before.

But Greta wasn't sure she liked the way the man looked at her. Hungry, almost feral, as if she was dinner and he a starving man. He clearly yearned for her, stealing caresses at every turn, eyes roving over her body with a fierce possessiveness. It made her uneasy to see. But the way they moved together – it was flawless. That she couldn't deny.

STRANGE AND TWISTED THINGS

Eventually the song ended and they vanished, the house suddenly too quiet. How had she ever wanted them gone? She needed them, needed them with an ache she felt in her toes, in her chest, in her lungs.

But she still wasn't alone. The shadow was back, glowing red eyes staring at her. She jumped so hard she almost fell, rearing backwards with fright. Heart pounding, she hobbled back up the stairs as fast as she could, careful not to leave her safe confines. She slammed the door behind her, locking it automatically, as if that would help against a ghost. She shivered, hands still shaking as she climbed into bed.

But even so. It had been worth it.

It quickly became part of her nightly ritual (the amount of salt it took was staggering, though she didn't care). She ached to see such beauty, to witness a moment so profound it echoed through time. It was magic, actual magic, and it was all hers. She felt almost as if it were a duty to witness it, something so important should not go unnoticed.

And so it became a sort of north star for her. She would count down the hours, sometimes she couldn't believe how long she still had to wait. Six o'clock, almost all the daylight gone and still she had another five hours to wait! By the time nine o'clock came she was getting antsy, worrying something terrible would happen and she would miss it. Ten thirty and she was pacing nervously, heart hammering, ready to leave her room in just a few moments, wondering if it was worth going down early, just in case. She never missed it once. It was too alluring, too important. That one glittering moment so incredible that she was happy to live for it, to allow her days to revolve totally around the dance. It was that good.

Even as she crawled into bed afterwards, she was anticipating the next day.

She knew she was mad. But she wasn't alone either, that graceful woman and that strange man keeping her company for just a few moments each night. And that was worth it.

Besides, who else was there to impress? It made her happy and it seemed to do no harm to them. Based on Violet's diary, she would probably like being admired so.

The days crept by, not peacefully exactly, but at least without incident. Mary-Beth was able to leave the hospital, though she had not returned any of Greta's calls. She wasn't surprised. How could they deny the truth now? She knew Greta had been right, and that was a lot to swallow. She trusted that in time, Mary-Beth would come around, either with rationalization or acceptance. She just prayed it was soon. She would wait as long as it took, but that didn't make it pleasant. Greta started to call, over and over again, multiple times a day. She knew it was wrong. Knew it was probably counter-productive, making herself an obligation, a weight instead of a friend.

But she didn't care. She just wanted to know her friend was okay. If it meant the end of everything, the end of them...well, it was what she deserved. Nothing was more important than just knowing, knowing if she was okay or not.

Finally, a text arrived. It had clearly been agonized over, its tone clipped and grammar perfect in a way they had never bothered with before.

"Greta," it read. "I understand that you are worried about me, but please stop. I don't want to discuss this. I need time and space. I will write you a letter – a real letter, in the mail, like we used to- when I am ready. Until then, I need space. Take care of yourself. Mary-Beth."

It felt as if a part of her soul shut down. She had a feeling she would never hear from that woman again, from her best friend, her confidant, her shoulder to cry on. Knew that Mary-Beth didn't quite have the courage to say 'goodbye', that it would always be 'later, later, later'. And Greta would be the one waiting forever.

But she wasn't about to give up. That was Mary-Beth's failing, she decided, squaring her shoulders. It wouldn't be hers.

So she developed a routine. Everyday, at two o'clock precisely, she would go down to the mailbox. She would open it slowly, as if hoping to creep up on the letter from Mary-Beth – too sudden and she would disturb it. Then, reaching far in, rummaging around so hard, so desperately she made the thing shudder and creak, she would find nothing. Or worse, her fingers would close around junk mail, and for one sweet moment she would believe, really believe, feeling sweet and cool relief, only for it to be shattered time and time again.

If only her leg didn't hurt so much. It was becoming stiff and hard, as if it wasn't fully alive anymore. She tried to exercise it, as if she could stop the pain by sheer force of will. It helped somewhat, she was sure of it. But still, when she had to manually force her ankle into position, she knew it couldn't be good.

She watched the sun set from her bedroom window, the sky alight with pinks and reds, great streaks marking the end of the day with one final show of glory. She found she was oddly glad to be cooped up in her room. She had never really noticed the sunsets before, though she knew she had hurried past thousands of them in her lifetime, too preoccupied to notice. She was relieved that now, at the end, that was changing.

And she was sure it was the end. She might still have half a chance if she could have the amputation. That had seemed to help the girl, but what doctor in their right mind would do that? She'd be carted to the looney bin instead. Or used as some kind of medical marvel. Researched and poked and experimented on. She didn't want that.

Instead, she began to get her affairs in order. It was more complicated than she first expected. At one point she had assumed that all of her wealth would go to her children, but when Frederick didn't insist on a family, she found she was relieved, and the years sailed past without them. Then she had assumed it would go to Frederick's family, he was always much closer to them than she had been with hers, and she had always seen it as their money, together. But now...

"Gosh, perhaps that boy is the best option," she said to Delta, who purred and rolled over, allowing her to scratch his chin. "Or I could be one of those insane old ladies that leaves her entire fortune to her cat. You'd like that, wouldn't you, you sweet widdle thing."

It was a good distraction, but it didn't help. In truth, she hated the idea of giving it all up to Mark and his side of the family. Perhaps she was just being selfish, snobbish even. But she had never seen them build anything. They hadn't even preserved anything, squandering any money they were ever given pretty much instantly. And this house was all she had left now. She wanted it to last, to see everything she had done be enjoyed, not be sold and torn down.

"But I suppose that probably would be best, wouldn't it?" she asked Delta, as if he were in her own head. "Tear this old palace down. Maybe it will dispel the ghost. Get rid of the curse, or something like that." She bit her lip. She didn't want to. She didn't want to start all over again, a new house, a new project, a new thing to fall in love with and have it all taken away. Surely, she didn't have to go through all that again.

She sighed, rolling over, having made no progress with her predicament.

Instead, she threw herself into making it happy. It being the house. She was convinced now that there were two beings that haunted it. One, the girl seemed harmless enough, sad even. As if she just needed someone to see her, to witness her remarkable life. And then the eyes, those red, glowing eyes…They sent a shiver down her spine, not least because she knew so very little about them. They were simply there, watching her, waiting.

Greta knew she was getting ahead of herself, getting lost in flights of fancy. But she couldn't help it. She became protective of Violet, feeling sure that she was a helpless victim in all this, doomed to suffer nobly, a casualty of the world in which she lived. She saw a lot of herself in that strange girl, saw a pulsating desire to be loved, to be needed.

And the eyes, Greta felt, must be the thing that did this to her. She hated them, blaming all of her ills on them, even the ones that had occurred far before she had arrived at the house. Her Father's decline in senility, her brother's uselessness. Frederick's abandonment. She wove a narrative so strong and all-encompassing that it felt like fact, as if she simply knew how all the world worked based on this small house.

The only piece of the puzzle, the only fact she felt she hadn't yet teased out, was how Violet got *here* – a small, coastal Italian town of all places. Traveling across the continent was no easy feat in those days.

But she wasn't about to let that stop her. Instead, she gathered up all Violet's things that she could, even contacting Davide and asking if she could buy whatever he old things still had in storage, just on the off chance they might be related to her. He didn't ask for payment, of course, he was too kind for that. Besides, as he quite rightly pointed out, it's not like she had asked him to hold onto them for her.

She was sure that Violet liked it. When the rest of the perfume bottles were returned, she began to smell roses in the air, as if someone wearing that scent had just walked out of the room. When she finally got her hands on the original cutlery, low murmuring could be heard at night, complete with the sound of silverware scratching plates, as if someone were having a dinner party just beneath her. She reveled in every new artifact she found, feeling the house sing with the energy it had lacked. It began to feel like home.

She didn't feel as if she were invading Violet's privacy when she read the diary, more that she were getting to know a friend. Each night she cracked it open, desperate to hear more of this glorious woman's story, hoping against hope that she would be okay.

Chapter Ten

April 12th, 1847

I should write more. I really should, because I'm afraid what you are about to hear is a convoluted mess, the story fractured. I am afraid this will all be rather sudden for you. I just haven't had the heart to explain everything. My future is so uncertain, so dark. I've even heard the word 'prison' bandied about. It makes my soul shiver. I know full well that is a possible fate for me, perhaps even one I deserve. And yet, I find I can't stop giggling.

I am sorry, I'm not making any sense. Let me start again, properly this time.

My wedding was very tasteful. I looked as beautiful in my gown as I imagined, and even Georgina (who hasn't spoken to me for months) pursed her lips in envy. Henry couldn't stop smiling, I think he really believed this was a good outcome for me. The poor dear. Even mother seemed happy, drawing me in for a close hug and saying "There. Now all is forgotten." It made my skin crawl for some reason. I knew exactly what she was referring to, and if she was still talking about, it wasn't exactly forgotten, was it?

But it was father who touched me most of all. He cried. He held me tight and said he was proud of me. That I was a good daughter. It made me happy then, now it makes me want to weep.

The ceremony was as one expects, and I fear I am running out of time, so I shall skip the details. (Except to say that the officiant sneezed in the middle and I will never forgive him for it).

And then came the reception. An early lunch, as is traditional. At his estate just outside of London. It was still a little cold, and so the gardens were not in bloom yet, a fact I found to be disproportionately disappointing. It was a touch early, of course, but nonetheless I had expected some spring bulbs to be open. Thankfully he was not such a miserly man to let his guests freeze and so some fires were lit, allowing us to be at ease as soon as we arrived. I will admit, that was kind of him.

My cake was beautiful, a masterpiece of white sugar delicately formed into ivy and roses. Of course, it wasn't to be eaten. No, as is tradition, it was put to the side, next to the ones belonging to his previous wives, each just as perfect as they were the day they were made. I don't know why we have this tradition, but we do. The women must wait to eat their cake. In hindsight, I think that's when I started to get angry.

Why did those women have to wait, to have their share? The guests had theirs, of course. My husband had his – his *third* wedding cake. But we, we three women were expected to wait until our 25th wedding anniversary to cut ours. None of the other ladies made it, and I simply knew I would not make it to mine. I knew it like I knew that dream was important – like I knew I'd been pushed in the forest. I just knew. The difference was that now, I was ready to admit it.

I really wanted that cake. But I put it to the side, as I had been taught to do.

The reception went longer than I expected, people seemed to genuinely enjoy the food and my 'husband' – have I ever called him by name, by the way? Well, it's Ernest. I wouldn't bother remembering it because it's not going to be relevant after today.

Ernest had invited a lot of his friends, some of whom were slightly more palatable than I had expected, a few I was even slightly warming up to.

But they were, of course, beginning to drink. It was still early in the afternoon, but, well, it was a wedding. So I smiled at them, aware that as a wife, it was not my place to criticize. Instead, I had another glass of wine myself. They were starting to get bawdy. Even my brother looked a little concerned, and he was usually the first to get involved in such escapades. Instead he stood at a distance, brow furrowed.

I couldn't quite hear what they said. Not at first anyway. But then, after some time, everyone could hear. Comments about me, about bargain cows giving good milk, about my misfortune being his gain. About how they would start to pray for more pretty young girls to fall – maybe then they could afford one too.

They asked him to tell them what my leg looked like, under my skirts.

I couldn't take it any longer, I wheeled myself out of the parlor and into the hallway, not looking where I was going, just wanting to get away. How I wished I could run up the stairs, or out the front door and down the few steps it would take to get into the garden. For obvious reasons, I could not. I chose the front room instead, where guests had not yet come. To my great displeasure, Ernest followed me. He called out to me, asking what was wrong. Asking if I was excited about tonight. I turned around to face him. He was so much taller than me now. How strange it is, to always be seated when these people – these men – tower around you. He smelt of alcohol already.

He walked forward, watery eyes staring at me. I backed up as far as I could, until I was pressed against the window, the curtain tickling my shoulder. It was old and ragged. Like him. He leaned over me, one hand on each of my arm rests, breath hot on my face.

"You're my wife." He said, matter-of-factly. "I will provide for you. And you will bring my life... pleasure."

I said nothing.

"Why did you come in here anyway?" he asked. "Eager to be alone are we? Don't you worry pet, we'll have enough of that." And he winked.

I care about beauty. I do. It matters to me. Grace and elegance and decorum. They are the balm of life. Without that, all is misery and bleak hopelessness. And I just knew that with him, I would be lost in a sea of darkness forever.

I can't quite explain what happened next. I only had one answer for him. I leaned from my chair taking the corner of the curtain and put it into the fire.

It went up in an instant, the flames rushing up the fabric, across the top, down again and into the walls in less time than it took me to remove my hand.

He let out a yell, loud enough to alter the party goers. They rushed in and...well, I'm afraid it gets boring for a moment here. I was carried out by my brother, who I must say acted extremely gallantly. The men tried to put it out with water, and eventually succeeded, although not before a good amount of damage was done.

I said nothing, I claimed to be too traumatized for words. I probably was. Somehow, I don't know how exactly, my family got the guests to leave.

Then the real trouble started. My 'husband' railed against me, telling everyone what I had done. I didn't try and defend myself, I certainly didn't tell anyone what he had said. They wouldn't have cared. He was a husband, it was his right.

It cost my family a fortune. Probably most of our money. But he agreed, finally, that this was a secret that would stay between the five of us (mother, father, Henry, Ernest and myself). In return, we would pay to have all the damage repaired, the marriage would be annulled under the claim that I was too traumatized to function as a wife and besides, it had not been consummated yet. I was to be sent to a nunnery.

I am back home now. Mother won't look at me. Father keeps trying to get me to talk, but I can't. Henry tries his jokes, and I try to smile for him.

I have this...rage inside of me. I am angry. But I am also so tired, and I find it so impossible to believe that anything will change. And so....I do nothing, literally nothing but stare out the window until I can't handle it anymore. Until I see no other option than to burn it all down. And then I...lose my mind.

The truth is, this has been coming for some time. It was almost inevitable. I should have said, before, I'm sorry. I should have told someone. Then, at the very least it wouldn't be such a surprise... I just thought if I pushed it down, if I forced myself forward, didn't acknowledge it...then maybe I could get past it. It didn't work like that. I was in mourning, every day. Both for what I had lost, and for what I knew was coming.

I am not sorry for what I did, although I wish it had not hurt my family so. How is it that everything I tried to avoid – shame, spinsterhood, a burden on my family, the permanent denial of children, has all come to pass?

I leave for a nunnery in the next week or so. It will take some time to be arranged. Not many will take me now, as the sisters are expected to work. Gosh, what will that be like? I can honestly say I have never had to work a day in my life. It was glorious.

April 14th, 1847

Georgina came to visit me. Ugh, how awful that girl is. She couldn't stop smiling. She didn't even try to hide her glee at my 'misfortune', making sanctimonious comments about how unlucky I was, to lose my leg and my husband in so short a time. She even had the gall to talk about the sin of vanity! As if she was innocent of that! She's not, I can tell you that for a fact. Nor of greed, nor of sloth. Sadly, she's not the first person to try and 'comfort' me so. God these people really are tedious. They talk of nothing but balls and fashion – their highest entertainment being to stab each other in the back. Was I really like that? I shudder to think....

Oh well, I have decided to bear it stoically. There's nothing else to be done really. I chose my path, recklessly and wildly, but I still chose it.

I suppose in some ways, it's a relief. I hated him. He was a lecherous drunk.

Still no leeches.

April 16th, 1847

Well, a place has been found for me. Mother wrote me a letter about it. I shall copy it here.

"Violet. You are to go to the Sorelle Della Redenzione e Della Misericordia. They have accepted you and are aware of your needs."

The what? Sorelle? That's Italian – I think? I'm not staying in England, then. I'm not even going to France. She knows I've actually been practicing my French, that I'm truly getting good at it. I don't speak a word of Italian! Oh this is some vindictive revenge on her part, I'm sure of it. Why else would she pick there, of all places?

Well, I guess I shouldn't be too surprised. It's probably the most remote and unreachable place they can find for me. Maybe it's for the best. Some sort of fresh start. I've been thinking a lot about what it means to be a nun. Perhaps it is what my soul needs. Was the amputation truly enough to remove the...issue? Based on my sleeping issues, I doubt it very much. Maybe prayer is truly what I need.

April 18th, 1847

I leave tomorrow. Henry and Father have been so kind. They gave up asking me why I did it a couple of days ago. And while they do speak to me as if I am a bit slow, I've found that I can't blame them anymore. Perhaps I am.

I don't seriously expect that I will ever see them again. It is possible, of course. I think we shall write. But I don't think they will visit me. I have been able to find an approximate location for the Sorelle Della Redenzione e Misericordia and it seems that they are essentially as far away from my home as you can hope to be without leaving Europe.

I tried not to think about that though. I just focused on them. We played games, and sang songs, all night! It was so much fun. Even mother played at the piano. I think she was pleased to see the back of me. Or perhaps she simply forgot why this was all happening. But I couldn't, not quite. Something was on my mind. I had found the first new leech that morning.

It was a surprise to find that I wasn't surprised. It seemed natural, in a way. This thing was clearly supernatural, why would a worldly cure like an amputation stop it? Slow it certainly. But stop, entirely? No, that always seemed a little too good to be true. God, please help me. I can do no more than dedicate my life to you in full service.

Please let this be enough.

Chapter Eleven

Greta groaned as she put the book down, adjusting her back. It was getting stiff – whether from natural or unnatural causes, she couldn't say, only that it hurt like hell.

For just a moment she had felt relieved that the amputation had not worked, fearing that a real cure was just out of reach for her. And then she immediately felt guilty. That girl had deserved better. She had to admit, the picture of innocence she had once imagined was now fading slightly. She burnt the man's house down? Of course, she could understand that it wasn't an ideal situation but really, that was rather extreme, wasn't it?

She could never imagine doing the same. She knew she would have meekly surrendered and accepted it, desperate to please. She wasn't proud of it, but it was her truth nonetheless.

Perhaps she was judging too harshly, she decided. He was obviously a very unpleasant man and Violet had not shared many details about him. It's possible what he had truly done was far worse than what she had revealed. And even that was bad enough. Still, there was something intimidating about someone who would snap so easily, change from passive one moment to a terror the next. Could that sweet girl have been responsible for some of the damage here, before Greta knew what she was doing? She hated to think so. But she couldn't stop herself.

As if summoned up by her very thoughts, that night, things got bad.

She was in a light doze when she first heard it. In fact, she had assumed it was part of her dream, the light pitter patter like rainfall on the open ocean. But it wouldn't let up. Finally she awoke with a gasp, just as a pebble hit her window. She staggered out of bed, her deformed leg making her slow and awkward.

It was with some amount of trepidation that she pulled the curtains back. But of course, there was nothing to see out there, only more pebbles being hurled at her. It was pitch black for one thing, and for another, well... it didn't seem like ghosts relied on visible bodies much.

She sighed, climbing back into bed, wondering why she bothered getting up in the first place. Still, it was worrying. What if it managed to break the window? What did it mean that it was looking for a new way in, a new way to torment her? Certainly nothing good, she thought as she jammed the pillow over her head.

This continued into the next night, disrupting the little sleep she got. She began to nap during the day, which she hated. Daylight was so precious to her, the only time she didn't have to be cooped up in her room.

But still, she found she simply couldn't manage without. And when the TV started to randomly turn on in the middle of the night, things only got worse. Without her rest, her world became fractured, unstable. She was forgetting things more and more, surprised to find the days slip by in sleep, the nights crawl past with nothing but worry and fear. She hated feeling so alone, wishing, pathetically, that Violet, or even the shadow itself would protect her. Hadn't she done enough for it? Enough to earn some morsel of consideration in return?

She accepted it though, as she accepted everything else the house did to her. It was worth it. She had never seen a place so beautiful, let alone lived in one. She felt a fierce pride engulf her. She had done it. The frescos were bright, almost shining under the light. The floors now kept meticulously clear of dust. Now that the windows had been cleaned, the whole thing was lighter, brighter, more joyful. Not only that, but she literally played with magic. Changing and experimenting with the house, watching as her actions- even indirectly- caused something extraordinary. She was fully aware that the violin only played at night because of her actions, that the air was only fragrant with perfume because she had retrieved the bottle. She was a part of it, a part of all this splendor. She had moved beyond what most people could even dream of. She would take the rough with the smooth.

Besides, she had never particularly wanted to enforce her own will on others, happily adapting to them instead. And so why should this house be any different? There were actually times when the hauntings brought a smile to her face. Imagine, something so powerful, so mysteriously potent, that it bends the rules of reality. How wonderful.

Why would she want to change that? She no longer had guests at night of course. And the eyes still induced a chill in her so intense it made her actually recoil. But the rest of the house, the girl...well, she was truly in love with them. And she was proud of that fact. Proud she wasn't afraid. Proud that she had so much to give. It justified her in a way. Proved that she really was happy to simply be with another creature, needing nothing in return. It made her feel noble, serene. She could take care of herself, she knew how to be happy, knew how to create what she needed.

If only she could sleep.

That was the worst part, now that her days were ruined too. Things began to get truly bad when music started to play on repeat. Not her beloved violin, no, she thought she could probably handle that. But Alexa, playing the same two or three modern songs over and over again. Songs she didn't even recognize and certainly had not requested.

She had no idea what to do now. One night she simply broke down. Not knowing what else to do, feeling more stuck than she ever had in her life, she gathered her valuables together. A brooch her mother had given her, a bracelet from Frederick, the first garnet necklace she had ever bought with her own money. Pretty things, she hoped. Things a Victorian girl might hold dear.

It was night, but she was reckless. She stormed out of her room and down the aisle of salt she recreated every night, her things haphazardly tossed in a bag. This she threw on the couch, outside of her protection.

She took in one long breath, unsure of what to do now.

"Please," she said finally, speaking into the darkness. She clasped her hands together, as if in prayer. It occurred to her, suddenly, that this was exactly what she was doing. Praying. "I know you can hear me...uh, great house. I have never tried to hurt you. I am here in good faith. I care for you. Please stop this torment, leave me be. Take these jewels as an offering. As a sign that I will happily give to you. Just please stop this madness. I can't rest, I can't think properly. I can't do anything if I don't sleep. Don't you like what I've done for you? Don't you appreciate how wonderful this house is now? How beautiful?"

There was no reply. She scanned the room, no eyes staring out at her, no shadows moving.

"I've done nothing wrong," she whispered, although that was cold comfort. Violet had done nothing wrong either, and it hadn't helped. She stood there for a few moments, waiting for a sign, for anything. None came.

Finally, leg hurting and whole body cold, she turned around, limping up the stairs. "I deserve better than this," she muttered, finally falling into bed once more.

She gathered her jewels up the next morning, feeling foolish, as if a ghost could be bribed with shiny trinkets. But it seemed to have heard her. Taped her to front door that morning was a note:

GET OUT

It read simply, in bright and bold letters cut from a magazine.

She couldn't take it. Crumpling the note into a ball, she threw it down the hallway, heart racing. She knew she had no right to be disappointed, to be hurt. But she was. Not even the devil wanted her, it seemed. She tried to call Mary-Beth first, of course, but that went straight to the answering machine, as she knew it would.

Knowing nothing else to do, nobody else to turn to, she called her brother. He picked up almost immediately.

"Greta!" he said, sounding happy for once in his life. "How nice to hear from you. I'm sorry about last time. I know I get a bit...protective about Nicco . But well, he is my son, you know?"

"Yes, yes, I understand," she said, and she did. Family was family, that meant something. Well, to her it did at least.

"What about you though, are you okay?" he asked. They didn't usually call for casual chats, so she wasn't surprised at the note of concern in his voice. It actually made her smile, the tension in her shoulders easing slightly. It would be good to talk, to let it out.

"I..." she swallowed, suddenly not sure what she wanted to say. "I have to say I've been struggling a little recently."

And she dove into a heavily edited version of events, claiming that it was her fault the electronics kept turning on and off, implying she simply didn't know how to use them. She hated it, hated how weak and stupid it made her sound. But the truth would make her sound insane, and she had to get it off her chest somehow.

She was surprised how much it weighed on her. Her voice cracked when she spoke of how exhausted she was, when she remembered how lovely it had been to have Mary-Beth there.

"Why don't you stay here for a few days?" Mark offered, "I promise I won't charge rent." She could hear the smile in his voice. He was a good brother. He did care. "Only for a few days though. Then you'll have to start contributing to hot water at the very least."

It was her time to smile now. Some things never change.

"That would be lovely, actually." She said, and she meant it. "Thank you." She worried for a second that the eyes would follow her, that she would somehow contaminate Mark's home too. She paused.

"But, well, I'm not sure – "

"Nonsense!" He boomed. "You've been through a lot."

She bit her lip. The eyes had never followed her before, and she'd been out of the house plenty of times. It didn't even disturb her when she'd stayed the night in the hotel, she remembered suddenly, after Delta's midnight run to the vets.

"Well...if you insist."

"I do!" he said, arranging to pick her up the next morning. She was, despite her better judgment, truly touched.

It was only when she was once more getting into bed, suitcase already packed to leave the next day that she realized – it was an odd conversation, well, for Mark at least. He had never before listened so patiently to her, and certainly never offered for her to come and stay. Even after Frederick had left her, when she truly had nowhere else to go, she'd had to practically beg. Before that, she had only ever visited his house a handful of times, and he hadn't moved in decades.

She pushed the thought down, hating that she was suspicious of her own brother. They didn't have the same values to be sure, but he was still her brother. She could trust him.

But something still didn't feel right. And the more she mulled it over, the less confident she was. She had never known a an otherworldly spirit use tape before. The shadow wouldn't have to, surely? It seemed much more, well, *ghost-like* to leave threatening messages carved into the wall, or perhaps on a mirror, hot and steamy after a long shower. Or simply just attack her, and it hadn't even attempted to do that in some time.

Besides, where would it get the magazines necessary to write a message like that? She actually giggled at this thought, imagining some eldritch horror sitting down with a copy of Vogue. She certainly didn't have any in the house, being much more of a book reader herself. She wasn't even sure if the entities here leave the confines of the house? She had never known it to do so. That's not to say it couldn't, of course, it was entirely possible that it roamed all the way down the street, or even teleported magically across the world, but well... it didn't fit with her experience, limited though that was.

So when the front door heaved open, the unmistakable heft of it scraping across the floor, she felt both terror and anger. There were rules here, established rules. She had tried to abide by these rules, done everything she could. And now the shadow could just change them? No. No she wasn't having that at all. It wasn't allowed.

She got out of bed as swiftly as she could, the scent of something awful wafting up to greet her. It was the scent of decay, of moldy meat and something putrid and foul. She gagged, clawing open the door with difficulty. It seemed that her hands were becoming stiff now, though she didn't know if that was from old age or The Ugliness.

Finally she made it out, making her way to the landing as silently as possible. She was just about halfway down the stairs when she heard it. Voices. Three male voices. They were laughing, throwing what seemed to be blood at each other, like children splattering paint. For a second, she didn't think they were real, she assumed they were part of the house, another strange ghost thrown at her. But then one of them slipped in the blood, his knees hitting the wood floor hard, sending an all-too-human crack of pain throughout the house.

These boys were flesh and blood.

"What do you think you are doing?" she screeched, her voice echoing throughout the entire house.

They looked up at her in horror, but only for a moment. Then came peals of laughter. Clearly they were unconcerned that they had been caught. They thought it the funniest thing in the world. One of them kicked a bucket of blood over anyway, unconcerned that she could plainly see them.

"Get out," she yelled at them. Though they tried, they slipped and slid in the still-wet blood, holding onto each other's shirts, the whole thing increasingly amusing to them.

"Sorry lady," one of them called at her. "Got to make ends meet, you know?"

"Gotta hustle," Another yelled out, sending her a cheeky wink.

But she had stopped paying attention. Because hovering – just above them – were the eyes.

Red and gleaming, brighter, hungrier than she had ever seen them before. She gulped, heart hammering once again.

The beast simply looked at her, tilting its head just slightly.

Waiting. For her.

Her blood ran cold as she understood what it was asking. And what the answer was. She straightened her back, hands clenched by her side. And nodded. The eyes seemed to smile. In an instant, the mirror shattered, glass exploding everywhere, the frame flying down the hallway. Now the boys were scared, their cackling turned to screams,

They raced towards the front door, still left open. Until it wasn't, until it banged closed, seemingly of its own accord. Trapped now, and with nowhere to hide, they split up, scattering like bugs. She could swear the eyes were laughing.

"Come here!" she yelled, although she couldn't be heard over the din. "The salt. There's some in the kitchen. You need to – " But it was no use. Besides, she wasn't sure how hard to try, how hard she *wanted* to try. She could sense their fear, knew it intimately, she had experienced it herself so many times before. Of course she wanted to help them. But she was angry too.

The chaos was overwhelming, bloody footprints now streaked across the house, that horrible smell still dominating, shards of glass everywhere. Her beautiful home in tatters.

The eyes didn't seem to like it much either. A roar unlike anything she had ever heard bellowed through the hallways. Somewhere between a scream and the mechanical sound of gears turning, it sounded like it came from hell itself.

Doors slammed open and shut all around them, with no discernible purpose but to confuse and upset. As if that were necessary. It seemed to be building up to something, however, for amidst the sound and fury, the floors began to move, tilting like a ship in a storm, throwing the children here and there. The blood swirled, rising like waves in the sea, flowing, no – charging, towards one of the boys, wrapping around his leg, pulling him down. He scrambled forward, madly trying to get away, but the floors were slick, slick with the blood he had spilt and it was no use. He was dragged into the parlor, out of sight. All that remained was a blood curdling scream.

Another boy finally found the back door and raced out into the night. She let out a little breath. One of them got away. She wasn't sure if that was a good thing or bad.

The last had finally gone silent. She knew he had not escaped.

Finally, all was quiet.

The sudden stillness made the hairs on the back of her neck stand up. She forced herself to breathe deeply, praying that the house was finally satisfied. It took a long time for her to speak.

"I'm going to have to call the police, you know," she finally said, as if breaking bad news. Not to the intruders no, but to the house. She knew it did not like to be disturbed at night, But, well…she couldn't just do nothing. People would ask questions. She waited as long as she could, until the night was not quite so thick, until it was more a subtle gray than deep black.

Finally, she called, and they came. There were a lot of questions, a lot of concern for her. It didn't take them long to find out what had happened, the boy that found the back door sang like a canary. To his credit, he did seem genuinely remorseful.

He told the truth of course, that the house was haunted, that there were glowing red eyes and supernatural powers there. No one believed him. They all assumed he was trying to cover up for his real crime – trying to scare her out of the house. As she had suspected, Mark wanted her gone. Had paid people to make her think the house was haunted. Apparently Mary-Beth had mentioned something to him, something about Greta's fear, and well…it seemed like too good an opportunity to pass up.

Her own brother. The thought made her sick. She would never have even considered doing that to him, the thought would have never occurred to her.

"What will happen to him? To Mark, I mean?" she asked the friendly-looking police woman. She held her breath, suddenly overwhelmingly nervous, despite the fact that she didn't even know what she wanted.

"Oh well, he'll need a damn good lawyer." The woman (girl? She hardly looked to be out of her twenties) said, her lips pursed. She seemed deeply affronted on Greta's behalf, a fact that made the old lady smile.

"They did quite a bit of damage to the house it looks like, not to mention your emotional distress. They could end up owning you quite a bit of money," she continued.

That, Greta didn't care about. She just wanted justice. Wanted it to matter to someone. Wanted someone official to say: 'Yes, this was a terrible thing that happened. No, you didn't deserve it.'

"And the others?" she asked.

That first boy would go to prison for some time, she was told in a somber voice. She didn't know how to feel about that. Of course, she wanted justice, but...was that really fair?

The second, the one who flew through the window, was hospitalized. A coma. They weren't sure if he would wake up.

The third, the one who stayed inside the house, he seemed to have disappeared entirely.

"I have no idea where he went." Greta told the police officer honestly. "It was all such a rush."

"Of course, dear" The kindly woman said, patting her on the shoulder. "I'm amazed you remember as much as you do. Some people just block it out."

Greta nodded, glad that her reasoning had been accepted so easily. In truth, she didn't know how anyone could forget the events as horrible as that. She knew, somehow, they would stick in her mind forever.

It was well past three in the afternoon by the time they had finished with her, and by then she was utterly exhausted. She had insisted on keeping to her regular schedule, of checking the mail exactly at two in the afternoon, just in case, still hoping against hope that Mary-Beth would write. It felt like a ritual now, although she had lost real faith, the movement itself still bringing her comfort. The police thought her a little mad.

They had been very considerate, but it was just so much to go over, so many questions to answer. And she wasn't done yet. She'd have to deal with the insurance as well, that window had been original to the house, almost two hundred years old and quite precious.

But it wasn't the main thing on her mind. That was Mark.

She was so angry at him. She wanted to rage and kick and scream, wanted to submit him to the same atrocities he had put her through. But at the same time...she just didn't. Didn't want to deal with it at all, didn't want to believe it was real. She found dealing with her haunted house immensely preferable to handling the fiasco with her brother.

Finally, after the sun had set and she had been exiled to her bedroom, she called him. She was surprised her tone was so flat and even. She had run through it in her head a thousand times, and each time she sounded righteous and indignant. Now she just sounded tired.

He wasn't brave enough to pick up the phone.

"I don't ever want to speak to you again." She took in a deep breath, as if to say more, but then...realized there was no more to say. She was done.

Chapter Twelve

April 19th, 1847

It's rather exciting, being on a train. Everything goes by so fast! I thought I would be more sad than I am, more frightened. But actually...I feel shockingly calm. I'm not sure if that is good. I feel that it's inevitable I will blow up again. In the space of ten days I have lost my 'husband', family, and future. I am speeding towards the unknown. Surely I will eventually have a reaction to all this, but in this moment I can honestly say I am indifferent. I am more interested in watching the English countryside speed by. It's a marvel! I have been on a few trains before, of course. But never this far and never this fast.

Henry is equally as excited as I am. I'm lucky that he has been allowed to escort me there. My mother wanted one of the servants to do it. Thankfully, she was overruled, our father looked dismayed at the very idea.

I squeeze his hand and smile as a house appears and disappears almost as quickly, a whole village coming and going in almost an instant. I am determined to enjoy this.

April 23rd, 1847

Ah! Dear diary, I confess I do not plan to write to you for some time. I'm in Europe! And best of all, my brother is clearly in no hurry to cart me off to the nuns. We have just arrived in France and he has announced that we can spend a few days in Lourdes! He winked at me and said "It'll be good for your health, after all." Ah! I shall take the waters there, like a proper lady, relaxing in one of the best hotels. Imagine this: a honeymoon with no husband! What could be better?

Ah, the joy I feel is profound. Something tells me this might not be the only detour we take on the way to Italy. I am truly lucky to have such a brother.

What if I run away here? Seek my fortunes on my own? I have heard of that happening, of women being able to make their own way. Suddenly everything seems possible! I am sorry diary, but I intend to waste not a moment of time with my head stuck in a book.

April 30th, 1847

Quick note: these waters do seem to do wonders for my leeches! I swear I haven't seen one since I arrived! And – better news yet – Henry has had a fake leg made for me. He says that getting around the convent will be impossible in my chair, and I quite agree with him. Apparently it's most unusual for a woman to have one, typically it's only soldiers coming back from battle. But, well. I do think it's better than this chair. I'm excited to simply *stand* again! Huzzah! Oh to be actually, truly happy! What a luxury!

June 1st, 1847

Well. It was good, while it lasted. I should have studied though, should have at least started to learn Italian. I'm not sure it would have made much difference.

I arrived here a few days ago, and I must say, it has not been easy. I'll start out with how the Mother Superior greeted me, that should give you some idea of how I am regarded.

She was nice enough to my brother, allowing us a tearful farewell where we exchanged many promises to write. I was already overly emotional, I must admit, so when she took me into her room and scolded me, I simply burst into tears. I will never forget what she said, how she stood with her back to the stained glass windows of the chapel, the late evening sunlight streaming through.

"There are three types of women who come here," she said, her voice heavy with an Italian accent. "First, the type with a true devotion to God, a genuine calling. These girls, I applaud. Second, the ones who have, through misfortune or necessity been called to God's work, and accept their place humbly. These girls, I respect. The third –" here she pursed her lips, as if she didn't even want to say it, "– had every blessing and opportunity in life and are here because they have squandered it, leaving their family no option but to hide their shame. These girls...must be corrected."

I was left in no disillusionment as to which camp I belonged.

She ordered the medics to do a full body examination of me, ostensibly to see if I had caught any diseases on my long travels, but I think it was really to verify that I had, in fact, lost my leg and that I wasn't simply hiding it somewhere. None of them spoke any English, and though most did speak a little French, they seemed distinctly uninterested in using it. Thank God I had the foresight to check my skirts for leeches. Thankfully, they found none. (The leeches did return as soon as we had left Lourdes, by the way. I must ponder that.)

They did notice how sickeningly vile my right foot had become. God how I hate their smug little faces. I'll spare you the details (of my foot, that is, I'll happily regale you with endless stories about how horrible everyone is here. I have a feeling I am going to find endless material). Thankfully, without another foot to compare it to, it didn't look quite so out of place, or at least, they didn't jump up and yell "you're a witch" so, thank God for small mercies. Do they still burn witches here? It seems like a ludicrous question, but honestly I have no idea.

I must learn Italian. But how? This isn't so much the type of convent where we go out and help people, more the type where we simply sit and pray. All day. It's not even easy to get out to write this, I have to slip away and hide. We are allowed visitors, at scheduled times, but of course, I have no one.

I am determined to end on a slightly more happy note, so I am pleased to report that the convent is at least beautiful, though not to my taste. The grounds are extremely large; apparently we grow our own food here. I have not had a chance to see them yet, as we arrived quite late. The convent itself is built around a large courtyard, where I am told we may pray and sew when the weather is fine. Grape vines crawl up the sandy walls, and the red roof looks almost jolly. If I didn't know why I was here I would think it most fine. I share a room with the other girls of course, the ones who, like me, have not yet taken a formal vow. I am given some privacy on account of my leg, and am able to make some quite wild claims about how I must "go and care for it." Of course, if they don't speak any English, they can't ask any questions! Ha! Got them! I know my turning the tables on them like this gives them no end of displeasure.

STRANGE AND TWISTED THINGS

That sounded horrible, didn't it? I don't mean it. I do want to be nicer. It's just that if they are to use this language as a weapon against me, why can't I use it as a defense?

June 4th, 1847

The people here are awful, awful, awful. The other nuns just laugh at me, all the time. My Italian is no better and so I just have to point and things and grunt. I have no idea what to do, so I just follow them around like a lost puppy. I mean they are right, I'm sure I do look foolish, simply aping everyone else. But I have no idea what to do. I am trying to lose my vanity, to not take it so personally. I do understand that it is a flaw, that it is unladylike and frankly totally unwarranted in my current condition. It's not easy, but I am trying. I just...don't really know how to do it. I don't want to feel small, and meek, and ugly. I don't want to give up.

And I miss home so much.

June 7th, 1847

I have had a chance to explore the grounds. They have a maze here, just like the one in my dream. I feel sick.

June 10th, 1847

The other girls watch me take my leg off at night. They see the stump, rubbed raw by the apparatus I must lug about with me. I hear them whisper in Italian, though of course I do not know what they say.

Are all my days truly going to be like this? I can't imagine it. Surely, I can't allow it, I must

Suddenly, Greta's head snapped up, heart pounding wildly. She had lingered too long in the living room, had underestimated how low the sun was.

Greta was out of her room at night, unshielded by her precious salt.

Before her, closer than ever before, Violet waltzed into the room, the violin bursting into life.

She was outside of her salted enclosure, exposed, unsafe. But more than that, she was closer. Close enough to touch them. Everything was exactly the same as it always had been, the music, the steps, the longing...but it felt so different now. So much more dangerous. So much more...attainable.

She knew it was a bad idea. Every part of her knew, knew that it would probably lead to some unbearable sorrow.

How could touching a ghost lead to anything else?

But she wanted. She wanted so desperately, so completely.

And besides, a wild thought suddenly seized her. Maybe, maybe this would stop the heartache. The two of them were so beautiful. Possessed of such a wild grace, a mysterious, otherworldly, breathtaking life force that Greta could never tame, that would never really be hers. But that she *wanted*. And anything, even more pain, suddenly seemed preferable to the endless days of grief she had endured up to that point.

She touched the ghost.

It was like an explosion. Heat ran up her fingers, her hand, up her whole arm, seeming, somehow, to attach to her heart. And then there was darkness, everywhere, not only black, but evil, somehow. This desire to simply destroy, to consume, to take and take and take and never stop, chaos and destruction suddenly a hedonistic goal.

It was overwhelming, it made Greta want to fall to her knees and scream with the force of it, with this thing that seemed to have crawled inside of her and split her soul. She tried to rip her hand away. She couldn't. It was inside her now, this horrible thing, stuck on her soul like a leech. She fought for air, suddenly feeling like her heart was about to beat out of her chest, this frantic fire dancing inside her.

*Violet couldn't all be bad, she couldn't all be evil, I know there is something else here...*she thought wildly. *No, no no no, please.* She forced her eyes open trying to focus, to clear her mind. To find anything good, searching wildly for some kind of light to drown out this darkness. It worked. She looked up at their wedding photo, one of the many dotted across the mantlepiece, and smiled. He had been so good. So intensely phenomenal.

Everything else might be evil, might be wicked and sinful. But he wasn't. She knew that. Everything else could burn.

"Everything?" asked a voice inside her. Somehow, she knew that voice belonged to the eyes.

"Anything," she whispered back. "But not him."

Finally, she ripped her hand away, her whole body shaking. The air in the room was so thick and heavy with something that felt like smoke, making it difficult even to move. Violet seemed unaffected, continuing her dance with the same sublime beauty she always had. Eventually she faded, leaving Greta to struggle to her feet, hobbling off to bed. The house was strangely still now, as if respectfully giving her space.

The next morning she was in agony, far worse than any other morning. But she felt different, too. As if she had just completed a marathon or climbed a mountain. She wasn't afraid of the house anymore. Something had changed. She wouldn't be able to tell you why that was, exactly. It felt more alive, a deep, dark pulse that hummed through the entire thing, wanting and needing. But she understood it a little better now, as if she had found her place within its cosmos.

She knew the boy in the mirror wasn't happy. That he was being tortured. More than that, she had a shrewd idea that if she did break the mirror, she would set him free. She felt the house smile when she didn't, when instead she ran her hand gently over the surface, winking at Antonio when he noticed her.

You wouldn't stop a lion from eating its prey, she reasoned with herself. Isn't that the ethical thing to do, these days? Nature photographers who refuse to intervene even when innocent life is on the line. She didn't see how this was any different. She wouldn't care if it was.

She was still able to be kind. And she often was, to Delta especially, showering him with toys and pouring every ounce of her unending love into him.

So it was heart wrenching when she had to let him go.

The first day that she couldn't bend down to give him his food, she knew it was over. She couldn't take care of him anymore. She called Davide, the one person she could think of. He was decidedly nervous, unsure what witch's bargain he was getting himself into.

But even his suspicious heart broke a little when she said goodbye to her cat, burying her face in his fur one last time, breathing in his soft scent. She held onto him as long as she could, slowly explaining his every want and need, what a crook of his tail meant, how he liked his belly rubbed. Finally, with no excuses left, she handed him over. She thanked him endlessly, just to keep him in the room really, to hold on a little longer. He insisted it wasn't an issue, giving assurances that yes, he and his husband really would be okay looking after him, and yes, they had been talking about wanting to get a new pet for some time.

She closed the door behind them with a heavy sigh. The house felt even emptier.

She did nothing else that day, nothing but sit and wait for her ghost dancers to come, Violet and that gorgeous, if sinister, man. Each breath simply passed time until she wasn't alone anymore. She was shocked at how long each day was, at how much crying a person could fit in. So much loss and despair trapped between sunset and sunrise. All she could do was endure it.

They came, as she knew they would. She hummed along with the tune she knew so well now, losing herself in the elegance and the music just for a moment. And then they were gone.

And the eyes were there.

She didn't run this time, didn't think she'd be able to. She was too tired. She didn't even flinch. She'd almost been expecting it, she realized at that moment. For the first time, she looked, really looked.

Glowing red eyes and a body which was all shadow made slightly real. And it was cold. It seemed to suck the heat out of the room, like nothing could be happy or safe while it was there. And as she looked, it's many shadows morphed into faces. The darkness and gloom it left in its wake taking on horrible, human expressions of torment and pain. A few she recognized – Antonio's, Mary-Beths', her own. Many she did not.

She didn't know if she was being brave, or had simply given up, unable to care anymore. Perhaps, a small and squirming part of her realized, she was even beginning to enjoy it.

It did not take a genius to notice that, as the days had stretched out since its last feeding, the house was getting hungry again. That one boy trapped in the mirror was a goal meal, but it couldn't last forever.

And so, she did the only thing she felt was reasonable – she bought it more food.

Not humans, of course, but animals. Chickens, lobster, snakes. Any live creature she could order online. It helped, and she was surprised to find she didn't mind doing it; in fact, she quite liked it. She had always taken pride in being a caring person. A giving one. To be able to nurture something of this caliber...it seemed like an honor, one she was determined to live up to.

One day, a very nice young woman with a kid goat arrived, commenting on how much room she had, and how happy the goat would be there. "Help you sort that garden out, for a start! So nice your husband doesn't mind, by the way." She mused, looking at a wedding photo Greta had hung. "Mine is forever complaining about the smell!"

"He can't stop me doing anything," Greta said with a smile.

And so she said goodbye to the nice woman, making sure her car was out of sight before she moved.

With a sigh, she opened the door to the basement. The goat bleated nervously beside her, nuzzling her leg with its soft, brown head. It seemed to sense that something was down there, something evil, because it bucked backwards, trying to hide behind her. Only then she did feel the slightest squirm of remorse. But she knew what it was like to be hungry. To be helpless, trapped, reliant on one person to help you feel alive. She couldn't abandon any creature, and that included whatever strange thing haunted the house, to feel like that. She had to feed it.

She didn't want to stay, didn't want to watch. But she knew she had to. Somehow, it seemed even more cruel to leave the poor thing alone in its last moments, and besides, if she was going to do this, she was going to do it properly, as she did all things. She wasn't going to hide away, to pretend it wasn't real. Not anymore.

The sounds the goat made were so horrific, she was shocked the neighbors didn't call the police. Blood splattered up the walls as it ran, desperately, down the hallway, trying with all its might to get away. The eyes chased after it, catching it, biting it, letting it go again. Playing with it.

She sat, watching from the top of the stairs, the door to the basement closed firmly behind her. The less she thought about the goat, the less it mattered. The house was everything. Was home. She wanted it to grow, to be strong, to be fierce and unashamed. She didn't care if it consumed the goat because she didn't care if it consumed her. The house was above all else, above her own ego, her own place. If it needed to do that to her, to eat her, she realized with only mild shock, she would happily submit. She hoped it wouldn't, of course. She was pleased to be its custodian, honored to be given the role of helpmeet. She wanted to do a good job. She smiled as she felt how happy the house was, how pleased it was to have a play thing, however briefly, before it ate. She knew she would not feel remorse again.

It dragged the goat into a side room, out of her view, and eventually, all was silent.

She acknowledged the house was evil, that it attacked people, took lives, sanity, safety. It just didn't seem to bother her much anymore.

But it also wasn't helping with The Ugliness. One day, while changing into her clothes for the day, a nice green jumper and blue slacks, she saw how far it had advanced. It now crept around her ribs, like a giant hand had grabbed her by the back. Only her chest was now untouched, still soft and pale.

She was out of time. Death was coming for her, and soon. Yet, she still had no arrangements in place, no plan. She could not simply let the house fall into ruin again, or worse, let it fall into the hands of someone who did not understand its ways. But she didn't know what else to do. It seemed an impossible choice – would she have to destroy what she loved, or leave it to someone else, and see it destroy them? Desperately hoping that the diary would have some words of wisdom, she threw herself into reading it, now the only real companion she had.

June 10th, 1847

....Are all my days truly going to be like this? I can't imagine it. Surely, I can't allow it, I must do *something*.

June 12th, 1847

I miss home.

June 20th, 1847

I think I may have made a friend! A new girl just arrived, her name is Sabina and she speaks English! English and Italian, so she can teach me while we gather vegetables for supper. Apparently she is a widow, and opted to retire here instead of finding a new husband. Terrified of childbirth apparently, and who can blame her. She says that this isn't a bad place, she'll teach me how to get the most out of it.

I certainly hope so, I've had to sneak off and wash my leg of leeches every single night. It's getting so bad that I can feel them wiggle on my skin as I hobble about the place, one leg heavy with the prosthetic, the other being sucked dry by pests.

I can't keep doing this. I need something to happen.

June 25th, 1847

Sabina has been as true as her word. My Italian is rapidly improving under her tutelage (*molto grazie, il mio carino, sei davvero gentile essere il mio insegnante*! That is probably terrible, but at least it is a start!) and best of all: I met her brother! Oh, what a different world this is when one begins to understand it. No wonder the mother superior watches us all like a hawk – really, in some ways we have more freedom than 'normal' ladies.

A number of noblewomen have retired here, their male relations still dropping in on them (some more faithfully than others). And what men they are!! They are clearly very relaxed here, the nuns are even allowed to be alone with them. And they have such power! So many titles come walking through these halls, so many strange and elegant fashions. Ah, how I long to wear proper gowns, do my hair as the noble ladies do. It would make everything seem so normal again. It would be like everything was okay.

My word, how conflicted I am. I want to be better than this. To be above vanity, to impress god, and to win back my health. I truly do, even though I…I have to admit I'm questioning that approach. He doesn't seem to pay attention to me. Doesn't seem to notice me at all. But still, I WANT to be better. I truly do, I can see how vapid Georgina and that lot are, and I don't want to be that way. I yearn to be more, to be witty and charming, to see past the trappings of fake baubles and glitter. To know the truth, to know…more. Besides, everyone says vanity is a sin, and can everyone be wrong?

But I don't want to be ashamed either. I have done nothing to deserve this, and still I suffer. There is NO crime in recognizing beauty, and there is no shame in wanting the best for yourself. I am not wrong for what I believe, what I want. Who I am.

And these two truths wage war inside me. Moment to moment, second to second I come to a new conclusion and righteously promise myself that this is the one I will stick to. I surely go through half a dozen a day, each hard won, each seeming to be the best plan yet- until I think of the next. It is exhausting. I have no peace, nowhere to settle, no ground beneath my feet. All is constantly shifting.

But I don't want to talk about this anymore. Already it is doing my head in. I can't even explain it properly without sounding like a madwoman. I fear I have not expressed myself well at all.

No, instead I want to tell you about a visitor I saw today.

Severino.

Sabina's brother is – ah, I don't even know how to put it into words. Everything I wish I could have married. Witty, handsome, rich, unafraid. Young. We didn't have long together, obviously, but I know I will replay those moments in my head for quite some time.

June 26th, 1847

I so wished that being a good nun would stop these horrible leeches. I really am trying. When I pray, I mean it. When the others laugh at me, I bow my head in humility. When I am in church I truly only think of God. Do I just need to be more patient? Have more faith?

I have to admit, it is somewhat more tolerable than last time. At least I have accepted it, at least I am not quite so afraid. I even tolerate the little bastards a bit better. Simply picking them off is an option, it's just that now I have to do it both at night and just after lunch. Besides, What am I to do? Get yet another amputation? How would that help – and who could I even ask for it? I dare not admit this to anyone.

I think I might be truly out of options.

June 30th, 1847

The strangest thing happened today. I was walking with Sabina, pretending to look for tomatoes to be used in that evening's supper (which always takes a very long time, I assure you) when she suggested we go into the maze.

It might surprise you (or not, depending on how astute you are) that I haven't ventured in there yet. That dream I had...it still haunts me. It was so vivid. And when it came, at the start of all this... I just couldn't shake the feeling that there was something sinister about it. I wish I had listened to that feeling.

Sabina darted inside, giggling. Feeling, I'm sure, that this would be the perfect place to hide away from the nuns. I followed, unable to resist. It was tolerable for perhaps a minute. But my leeches... They didn't like it. That's the only way I can describe it. They become excited, writhing and moving under my skirts as if distressed. It was horrible. They are so wet and jelly-like, so awful to touch, let alone feel them crawling all over you (they shouldn't move like that! It's unnatural!). And then it *hurt*. Hurt beyond anything I can possibly tell you, like the bones were being pulled through my skin and out of my body. I couldn't take it. I fled.

I told Sabina that I was afraid on the uneven ground, that my stump leg couldn't take it. She didn't ask any questions, she has always been so very sensitive about that, so kind to me. All she did was give my hand a quick squeeze and say "Carino mio, it will all be okay. Try not to worry." But still, I'm not sure she entirely believed me either. What could this possibly mean?

Chapter Thirteen

Word spread fast in her little village. Only the next day, Davide came to check on her, more baked goods in hand. A Panettone this time. She beamed as she opened the door, glad to see a friendly face. It felt so normal, to have neighbors dropping in on her like this. It wasn't a routine, exactly, there was no set pattern. No it was easier than that, more fluid and casual.

"Hello dear! How are you? Would you like a cup of tea?" she asked, taking the box from him.

He ignored her.

"Are you alright?" he asked instead. She couldn't help but notice he didn't try to come inside.

"Oh yes. Thank you for asking. Not much damage, I think I've cleaned the blood up well enough, I had help from the police of course, but they – "

"Yes," he interrupted, wincing at the thought. "I uh, heard all about it already. Giulio was saying – "

"Giulio?" she asked, her head crooked to one side.

"Yes. One of the boys that was here. The one going to prison. His family has been living in this area for god knows how long," he said, as if that detail should clear everything up for her.

"Oh. I see," she said, wondering where all this was going.

"Well…he said he saw…eyes. Glowing red eyes?"

She sucked air through her teeth. She was so used to being simply dismissed as a fool, she didn't know what to say when asked about it directly.

"Yes…." she said. "I think I heard him say something about that." Her voice gave nothing away. She was proud of that.

"You know…as I mentioned, I grew up around this house. We used to have a game. Sneak in and see what you could take. Not a very good game, I know. But…there were rumors then too. Just kids freaking each other out, I thought. But I went in one night. Wanted to prove how tough I was." He was quiet for a moment, lost in thought.

"I saw red eyes then too."

Her heart leapt, thinking for a moment that maybe she might have an ally, someone to believe her. But then he spoke again.

"I don't understand how you live here." He said, obviously choosing his words carefully. "I've never really understood….it's a big task, on your own. And that's without…" He shrugged his shoulders, not knowing quite how to put it.

"The boys said you were screaming at them. Yelling at them to get out. Or cursing them, they couldn't tell," he said finally.

"Well, yes, but – " she started.

"Here." He said, thrusting the desert towards her. "Giulio isn't exactly a trustworthy kid, but…what he says tracks. Fits a lot of the legends that have always swirled around this place. And from the look in his eye…he's not making it up. If you didn't know the rumors before now…then I'm sorry for you. If you did, or if you decide to stay even though…Well, I don't think anyone will trouble you again."

And with that, he turned on his heel and left, not even stopping when she called out to him.

So she was finally, utterly alone. No husband, although that was old news now. No best friend, a fact she still held herself accountable for. No brother, although that may be a blessing. And now, no kindly neighbors, not even the hope of more to come in the future.

She had never felt this way before. It was awful. She began to keep a diary herself, although it was half a 'how to' guide for anyone who inherited the house next, and half rambling letters to Frederick, telling him all about her days. It was a poor substitute, but it did help.

Besides, she was resting better now. So, so much better, now that there were no pebbles at her window, no strange sounds. The only music was the one she craved: the violin with all its subtle elegance, and the dancers that accompanied it. Them, she visited every night, so excited each time, so enthralled, despite the fact that they never changed. They didn't need to. They were perfect.

The police had explained it all to her, how it was possible to hack into people's wifi these days, do strange things with their electronics. Of course the pebbles were no mystery, anyone with a good aim would be able to chuck things at her window. She didn't care. Strange things happened often enough around her, she just wanted peace.

Well, to be honest, she wanted what her ghost had, Violet and that strange man. The way they moved, so perfectly in time with the music, so in sync with each other. It was the highlight of her day, seeing them.

And it was becoming easier too. The few nights after the break in having no hauntings whatsoever, as if the house were napping after a good, filling meal.

And she had no doubt that's exactly what it was. For the first time, she felt its power during the day. She was cleaning the old mirror (miraculously fixed, no cracks or even scuffs marring its smooth surface) in the front hall when she saw it. Of course, she thought she was imagining it at first, her rational side still not entirely conquered. But when it happened a second time, she had to accept it.

Looking at the mirror in the right way, in the right light, it wasn't her own face staring back at her, but Antonio's – the boy who had vanished. She had learnt his name from the many 'missing' fliers that now dotted the town. His family assumed he was on the run, afraid of the consequences of his own actions. He wasn't always visible, but when he was, he was fractured, his face contorted in rage or fear, mouth open in a silent scream. It didn't concern Greta overly, a fact she was actually quite proud of. She was getting used to the house and its strange ways. She was getting stronger, more resilient.

"Well, what am I supposed to do with this?" she asked the mirror, and for once she wouldn't have been at all surprised if it had answered back. It didn't.

"I will talk to the house about you, but it doesn't seem to really listen to me," she said, wiping it down. But then, she realized, hadn't her problems cleared up directly after she asked the house for help? The very next day, in fact? Perhaps that meant something.

God, it was impossible to tell if these things were coincidental or not. It drove her mad, wasting away her time simply worrying. She considered smashing the mirror, to release him in some fashion. But would that help, or hurt? Would Antonio be released to rest peacefully, or to haunt her forever? Was he a ghost now? Surely he was not still alive, not in the traditional sense anyway. Would smashing the mirror be like killing him? She couldn't stomach that.

So life went on. She adapted well enough to having yet another supernatural entity around. It seemed he could not leave the mirror, so sometimes she set up a portable TV for him in front of the mirror, setting it up to play cartoons. She assumed that's what kids liked. She hoped it helped him.

"I wonder what will happen to my soul, when I die," she mused aloud to Floppy, arranging a vase of flowers – pink roses and deep purple lilacs, her favorite.

"I don't think being stuck in a mirror is all that bad. At least you got to see the world go by; at least you weren't being tormented by demons, or dipped in fire. At least you could see people's smiling faces, helping them primp their makeup or adjust a tie." She continued, hoping Antonio could hear her, that it would give him something to think about.

She would be quite happy in a mirror, she reflected.

She was much more afraid she was going to become a wizened old hag, some kind of undead monster. The Ugliness, as Violet called it, had spread far throughout her body. It was so strange, as if she were already partly mummified. Her skin tough as leather, the joints hard to move, her whole body coarse and dried.

It had spread to both legs now, and up her arms. She hated to think she would happen when it got to her chest. A heart attack, she assumed. That seemed almost preferable to becoming a ghoul, which now seemed like a strikingly realistic possibility.

And she still had not figured out her will.

Who to leave this to? Mark and his side of the family were very clearly out. She sighed, wondering if she had the stomach to leave the house to Frederick. It seemed that he would unfortunately outlive her, unless he was also dealing with some horrific curse she didn't know about.

She could tell her time was running out. Moving was so awkward now and each thing she did had to be a deliberate choice, thought out well in advance. She was just glad she could still take care of Delta, who never seemed to waver in his loyalty.

"I love you," she told him, out of the blue one day. It felt nice to say it, though she knew she would get no response. He just headbutted her hand, purring away. She liked it. It made her feel special, as if he needed her. Appreciated her.

But it was easy to open the diary, to sit with it perched lightly on her lap, to feel the dry pages beneath her fingers. She had got used to Violet's spindly handwriting long ago. So it was with a sense of happy excitement that she sat down to read once more, nestled happily into velvet couch cushions, a cat by her side.

Chapter Fourteen

Greta had now taken to carrying Floppy around with her everywhere, the days where she worried about looking foolish were now long past. Stuffed under her arm or held lightly by the wing, he was truly important to her. If anything, the house seemed to find it amusing, that such a small, insignificant object was the recipient of all that love.

Sometimes, it threw Floppy around, made him fly down the halls or hop down the stairs. It stopped when she cried though, returning it to her as you would a toy to a child, wiggling it in the air. And soon, when she learned it *would* stop, she didn't cry any more. Just accepted it as it was, coming quickly to peace. Besides, a part of her liked it. Liked Floppy being just a tiny bit alive. That way, she could tell herself she didn't live alone. That mattered to her.

She'd had a lot of time to think about all that, about what was important, and she was surprised to find that frankly, dignity was not very far up there. She was willing to try anything now, willing to explore, to consider things she never would have a few short months ago.

Willing to go into the maze.

In all honesty, it frightened her more than the house. She didn't know why, perhaps it was because the house was so well known to her now, or perhaps because she hated the idea of being trapped. Whatever it was, she had avoided it like the plague.

But now, it seemed like she had no option. If the diary was teaching her anything, it was that the maze was important. If it had affected Violet that badly, what on earth would it do to her, with The Ugliness so far advanced. Greta hated to think. But she couldn't avoid it much longer, she knew it was, perhaps, the one place she could find real answers. The only lead available to her. She spent hours plucking every leech off of her. In truth, she hadn't realized how haphazard she had become with them. They didn't bother her anywhere near as much as they bothered Violet, and though she did remove the most obvious ones each morning, she couldn't easily reach her back, and 'out of sight, out of mind' was her motto. She made sure to take some pain killers as well, not a lot, but hopefully enough to make a difference. Although what exactly would make a difference to ancient curses, she couldn't say. She just thought it was worth trying.

And so, late one afternoon, she set off, shoulders straight and back determinedly straight.

She wore her wedding gown.

She told herself that there were practical reasons for this. That beauty was somehow part of all of this, that the house had (maybe?) accepted her offerings of jewels, and that perhaps that meant it liked the finer things.

But also because it made her feel pretty again. And maybe that was enough. She hadn't worn it since that day, since her mother had done her hair and her father walked her down the aisle. She had been so happy then. And so why not wear it? Nothing seemed to matter anymore. It made her smile, to feel its soft silk on her skin, the heavy skirts swishing as she walked. She beamed with pride that it still fit. She even donned the pearl earrings again, the droplets grazing her neck. She felt fantastic.

And that was how an elderly bride walked into the garden, breeze lifting the delicate lace at her waist with a soft sigh. Her dress rustled in the grass, brushing against the wildflowers and crinkling across the fresh fall leaves.

The maze had such a sinister allure. It was a marvel to her that it was still a maze at all, and not simple a mass of overgrown hedge. Surely no one had taken care of it in years, probably decades. But then, she supposed, far stranger things had happened in this house.

With a trembling hand, she reached out to touch it, wondering if that alone would be enough to induce the crippling pain Violet spoke of. It wasn't. Casually, she took a step inside. And another, and another, no ill effects obvious at all.

That was almost more concerning, wondering if it would suddenly all leap upon her at once. Or perhaps that power had withered somehow, did curses die of old age? Or maybe it had been vanquished by some noble hero. She smiled, suddenly feeling lighter. Yes, that must be it. All fairy tales had their hero, and what was this apart from a fairy tale? She said a silent thank you to whatever force allowed her inside and pushed on.

Finally, she came to the center of the maze. Before her stood a statue. Aphrodite would be her guess, something vaguely Roman at least. Or maybe Greek? She had never been able to tell them apart. Just that it was old, and it was beautiful. Its pure white marble was handsomely carved, the woman's naked breast only just covered by her long hair. She stared, unseeing at Greta, a sword in one hand and shells at her feet.

"Hello" Greta said, no longer afraid of her own voice. There was no response, but perhaps she had become too acclimated to Floppy, because this didn't phase her. She simply continued.

"My name is Greta. I wish I knew yours. Are you the eyes? I know you're not the poor boy in the mirror, but – can he hear me too? Can he travel here?"

She sat down on the iron bench that sat across from the statue, enjoying fanning her skirts out. It was only then she noticed a few words stamped into the metal.

"To my sister, Sabina. 1815-1866. May you rest in eternal glory, unafraid and unyielding."

What a strange thing to have here, she thought. And then she realized it wasn't strange at all.

It was peaceful here, so much more than the house. The birds still sang, even at this late hour, the air was heavy with the scent of flowers. It was lovely.

But no other wisdom came to her, no half of inspiration, no answers. She felt foolish for having resisted it so much, it was so clearly harmless. She stayed as long as she dared, playing a game of chicken with the sun, seeing who would go to bed first.

She did, of course, being still weary to traverse the house freely at night. But still, it was a close call, closer than she'd ever left it before. The very first stars were out by the time she was inside, dusk having fully fallen.

She was just getting ready to start the next day when a call interrupted her.

"Davide," she said, delighted to hear from him. But then: "It's not Delta is it, he's okay?"

"What? Oh, no. He's great, loves how much sun we get here. Uh no, that's not what I'm calling about," he said, a little breathlessly.

"What is it then?" she asked, spreading jam on her toast. "Everything all right?" She missed the man, missed the nice little chats they used to have.

"Well...some of the other neighbors have been a bit, uh...spooked, recently. They say they hear music coming from your house in the middle of the night. Live music? But always the same.... They know you get animals delivered but, well...they don't know where they go."

"I eat them," she said, a little too quickly. But really! What a stupid question, as if they were all vegetarians themselves.

"Alive...?" he asked.

"No, of course not!" she said, momentarily thrown. Was that really what they thought of her? That she wolfed down live lobsters like some kind of animal? She didn't know if she should laugh or scream. She settled for a little bit of each which doubtless made her sound even more insane. "Who's asking anyway?" she demanded. "What, do you all have some kind of committee to keep an eye on this? On me?"

"I mean we, uh, well... But no – that's not the point! The point is, there has been concern for some time and... well last night someone saw... Well, I can't believe I'm saying this. But they saw... a ghost?"

"Oh yeah?" she said, momentarily forgetting this was supposed to be a major revolution. "I mean uh, surely not." She was making a half-hearted attempt to be anything but what she truly was: an old lady in a haunted house.

"Yes, some kind of...woman in white?"

Greta roared with laughter, harder than she had in years, her ribs aching, head thrown back in joy. She hung up the phone, having no time for these people; they had no idea what they were talking about anyway. He could call her back if he was that concerned. He didn't.

After that, she made a habit of donning her wedding dress and stepping out into the night. She liked the idea that she was spreading a little mystery in the world, enjoyed the thought that somewhere, people were whispering about her.

She even dared the darkness of the house to do it. Her time was close, and the eyes were well fed. She could just tell it liked it anyway, enjoyed the chaos and fear she was spreading in the night. It wouldn't hurt her, not then. She had even bought a new veil, especially thick, to hide her face in, lest a nosy neighbor get too close and ruin the fun. She couldn't have that. She wasn't sure if people would be more or less afraid to know it was a mad old lady that haunted the village, but she liked to keep the mystery alive.

When she went into town and people gossiped in her wake, she smiled. Somehow, it all seemed so incredibly funny. She amused herself by muttering curses under her breath, scaring local children. Her reputation certainly preceded her.

"Oooo, I wouldn't do that my dear" She hissed at some random woman about to buy a jar of olives. "Not the right time. The moon wouldn't like it, see. Not the right time at all...". She shook her head wisely, and the woman, now pale as a ghost herself, raced out of the store, not even buying the bread she had been carrying.

Greta bought the olives herself. They were the last on the shelf, after all.

And so it was, on a wet, chilly evening, that she stood in her bedroom, just putting the final touches on her wedding outfit. It was then that the doorbell rang. She swore loudly and looked out the window, trying to see who was there.

Mark. Standing there, on her front step, as if it belonged to him. As if he had the right.

Suddenly her heart was pounding. She didn't care how she looked, didn't care how she was dressed. She just wanted to hit him, wanted to hurt him for what he had done to her.

She stomped down the stairs and threw the door open with more force than she knew she had, furry welling up inside her.

"What do you want?" she demanded, not bothering with a hello. He wasn't worth it.

For one moment, he stood there, mouth agape and eyes wide.

"Is that your wedding gown?! You've lost it," he said, looking her up and down. "You've absolutely lost it."

"And you're a bastard," she shot back. "Is that all? I'm rather busy, you know."

He stared at her.

"Well," she said, taking a long breath. "Thanks for the visit." But before she could close the door, he brushed past her, forcing himself inside.

"Uh no. Don't think you are getting rid of me that easily," he said, stomping through to the dining room. For a moment she held her breath, wondering if he would catch sight of Antonio in the mirror. But either he was incapable of that, or far too distracted, not seeing the other face that briefly screamed at him. Instead he headed over to her drinks table, pouring himself a large brandy.

"Want a drink?" she offered tartly.

He ignored her. "Why on earth would you want to hold onto a place like this? It's massive, you know. Massive! I bet you have barely even been to the top floor. Bet you can't go to the basement these days, not with the stairs. It's selfish, that's what it is, selfish."

"I'm the selfish one?!" she screamed. "I'm not the one that tried to scam their own sister! Do you have any idea what that did to me?"

And they were off, volleying back and forth every time they had ever hurt each other, going all the way back to childhood, each feeling confident they were winning.

STRANGE AND TWISTED THINGS

So Greta didn't notice the lengthening shadows, or the clock strike the hour. Didn't see the moon come out, didn't notice the dimming light. Not until it was almost completely dark.

"You need to get out," she said finally, her voice hoarse and frail.

"Not until you do the right thing. You've always done this, always hoarded your treasure for yourself, just because you were luckier. That's all it is, you know, luck." he said, working himself up into a frenzy once more.

She didn't bother to warn him again. She didn't particularly want him to suffer, but she did want the house to be well-fed. She wanted it to be happy, to have its little toys. It clearly liked to play, after all, didn't it play with her and Floppy?

And then the eyes, glowing a deep primal red, hovering just behind him.

"You should go..." she said, no effort or passion in her voice, only apathy.

But he wasn't listening. He never listened to her. And now she realized, he never would. She accepted this, like she accepted most things, quickly and quietly. She left him to himself. She did lock the door, both the front and the back, and she did unplug the land line phone she was still old-fashioned enough to have. She felt proud of herself for thinking of that, and somehow, deep down, she knew the house was proud of her too. It seemed to hug her, that same heat from before wrapping around her chest. But it felt good this time, pleasant. It could easily kill her, snap her in half like a twig, or throw her down the stairs. But it didn't. And she knew she had done a good job. She couldn't help but smile.

She climbed up the spiral staircase, calling out once last time: "You really should go." Though her voice did not carry to the dining room, as she knew damn well it wouldn't. She didn't really know what else was expected of her at this point. It occurred to her, of course, that maybe she should put a little more effort in. But she thought of Mary-Beth, how impossible she had been to convince. It would take far more time, and much more energy than she had, to convince a man as stubborn as Mark. She tucked herself into bed, cuddling her trusted Floppy as the screams started. She found herself glad the house was eating well, having fun. She only hoped it didn't leave a mess.

She wondered if this made her a bad person or not. She decided that yes, yes it did. She laid back, the stuffed owl on her chest, arms wrapped snugly around it. *I kept Floppy safe,* she thought. *I protected Delta too, at least after the first incident. I did what I could. Can they ask for more?*

She had just become so tired. So tired of always having to be the bigger person, of having to be compassionate. Not for the first time, she longed for someone to be that way with her. Ever since she was a little girl she had dreamed of big romantic gestures, of grand statements. Of love that would last through time, just like her precious ghosts.

If she were to haunt this place, she suddenly realized, she would do it alone.

That hurt worse than losing her brother. Far worse. And that was when she realized that yes, yes: she was truly a bad person. And there wasn't anything she could do about it.

"Perhaps that's why everyone left," she said to Floppy, the soft fur on his head tickling her lips. "Perhaps I deserved it."

Eventually the screams stopped. They didn't fade into the distance, they didn't calm down. They stopped, suddenly, brutally. She knew what that meant.

She would spend the next few days looking for her brother, checking mirrors, listening at the basement door, peering into the shadows. Anywhere in the house she thought a lost soul might settle, which didn't exactly narrow things down. She was curious, and besides, she didn't think it was good for either of them to have him just floating about. He needed a home, like the mirror, that she could care for.

It was only when she was dusting that she found 'him'. Pulling out some books from the library shelf, one fell open. His favorite, the one their mother used to read to them as children. She had almost forgotten it by now, something about dragons and mermaids, a prince that gallops in to save the day.

Mark clearly had not forgotten though. His voice flowed from the pages, nothing coherent, no one phrase in particular. It was like all the words he had ever said were contained in that book. She could make some of them out 'sister', 'money', 'fair', 'only right'. But it was more a cascade of words than anything comprehensible. With a sigh, she snapped it shut, and put it back on the shelf.

She knew, she had always known, that if he only let her care for him, had just taken her advice, actually listened, then all would be well. Now, he would have no choice. He was at her mercy. Mercy that she had in limitless supply. She would make things as good as could be.

So it was with both surprise and the smallest amount of hope that she opened her front door one day – to see her nephew, Mark's son, sitting there. Waiting for her.

Chapter Fifteen

July 2nd, 1847

I do genuinely wish God would help me, and if he did, I would welcome it as a true miracle.

July 5th, 1847

It has been one year since all this began. One year to the day. I went back and read that first diary entry. I wanted to laugh. I cried instead. Am I truly a terrible person? Surely I am no worse than Georgina, who herself is not bad at all. Vapid and thoughtless perhaps, but bad... no. I do not deserve this, and if God, in his infinite wisdom, pushes me into the hands of the devil.... Well that's his choice, isn't it? I can't know his mind, can't guess his will. All I can do is try and protect myself. And this clearly isn't working.

July 7th, 1847

I do not think I have ever been in worse agony. Perhaps that is only because the amputation is now a distant memory, but this, this

STRANGE AND TWISTED THINGS 161

is horrible. This burning sensation, my whole body raw and feverish and on fire.

I had an idea. Like most of my ideas, it was a double-edged sword. It occurred to me that if the leeches do not like the maze, perhaps that is because the maze could hurt them. While Sabina and I were out yesterday, I surreptitiously picked some leaves from the outside of the maze. That night, I picked the leeches off using them. They hated it! It was a glorious moment watching their small bodies write and hiss, I knew they were in pain and I loved it. Perhaps that is why God has rejected me. I have no compassion for these vile things that crawl across my body without my consent. I hate them, and I want them to suffer.

But that is not the point. This morning, for the first time in a long time, there were no leeches upon my leg. What a burst of joy I felt, what a searing pulse of relief. I had to bury my face in my pillow, hide my smile, I was so overjoyed. It was short lived. Throughout the day, the burning has become worse and worse. I can see, traced down my leg, where I used the leaves on my skin. Long lines of now blistering red criss-crossed across my thigh. My hands too, I claimed I spilled boiling water on them, and thankfully no one cares enough to check.

I am so exhausted, so sick of this. But I have no other choice than to move forward. The leaves did help. They have not come back yet. I can repeat the process when necessary. And that alone is more progress than I have made in a year.

July 20th, 1847

It is a hard decision to make, the leeches or the burning. But at least with the burning, it is my choice. I am in control. And so that is the one I have been picking the most often. It has occurred to me that the maze may hold yet more answers for me. I mean WHY does it react like that? Why did I dream about it? Why does it hurt my leeches? Could it possibly be more holy than the chapel we have here, the one that is filled with praying nuns practically every moment of the day? How would that be possible?

But if it's not more holy, if it's not God...what is it? I need to find out. I need answers.

July 22nd, 1847

I tried, in my broken and child-like Italian, to ask one of the women here what they knew about the maze. She couldn't help but snigger. She rolled her eyes and spoke as slowly as possible, as if to a child. It actually helped quite a lot, I don't think I possibly could have understood her otherwise.

Sadly, she knew nothing of note. She told me stupid things, like how its big, and green and easy to get lost in. I can see all that, I need to know about its history.

July 28th, 1847

I have asked a few more girls, the kinder ones. Sadly, they know nothing. I dare not ask more people, or more openly, for fear that if there is something...untoward about the maze, I shall be found out. There is clearly some evil here. I can't help but wonder what they know. Who knows. I find I am becoming suspicious, surely it can't be coincidence that this monastery was built here. Are we supposed to be the guardians? Keeping something locked away? Or have we failed somehow, and let an ancient evil creep in?

I am afraid that I am going to have to go to Mother Superior's office. She had books there, I saw them when I arrived. And surely, if anyone knows, she does?

August 1st, 1847

I have not eaten in days. The heat is unbearable. And the leeches crawl across my whole body with impunity. It has not been easy to write recently, I am watched day and night, and so this will have to be quick. I will try and snatch what little moments I can, you are the only thing that keeps me sane. The only one I can be honest with. I have something...very stupid to confess to you.

I knew it was foolish to try and go into her rooms without permission, but what choice did I have? Sitting and doing nothing simply is not an option. I truly believed it was the only path open to me.

And so, that night, I crept down the corridor. I should have known even then this was a foolish task and turned right back around. Have you ever tried to sneak about with a prosthetic limb? This hunk of wood is heavy and hard to control. I could take it off, of course, try to hobble about on only one foot, but that hardly seemed dexterous.

Besides, I was afraid I would have to run.

Getting there was relatively easy. A full moon shone down into the courtyard, illuminating the vines with a soft, silver glow. If I hadn't had other matters on my mind, I would have stopped to admire it. It must have been about then that my thudding alerted someone.

But I wasn't to know that at the time. Instead, I scurried forward as best I could, slipping down the stairs and into her rooms. It was pitch black, no light coming through that stained glass window I had once admired.

Her desk was heavy with paper, letters here, ledgers there, accounts and records spread neatly across the pages. Frankly, I was dying of curiosity, wondering if any of it was about me. If, perhaps, my mother had written to inquire (she never writes to me directly). But I knew that wasn't the point.

Instead, I drew my gaze to the rows and rows of books that lined the walls. I lifted my candle to them, the light glinting off the well-worn spines. The Bible, of course. And many titles like it, including multiple copies of *A brief outline of the evidence of the Christian religion* by Archibald Alexander. I was just about to pry out a promising looking tome, on the history of convents in Italy, when the door banged open.

Mother Superior stood there with a such a look of rage, I have never seen anything like it.

"What do you think you are doing?" she bellowed, marching over to me and grabbing me by the arm. It was lucky my candle didn't tip, light something on fire. I knew how easy that was, now.

But rational thought such as this seemed to be the last thing on her mind. Her eyes were wide with rage, her lips thin with it. Her whole face was twisted and spiteful, as if I had wounded her personally, deeply just by my presence. I hung my head in shame, but it did little.

She yelled so long and loud, I'm shocked she didn't wake the entire convent up. She probably did, I'm now realizing, my whole world blisteringly aware of my shame.

She raced from loud, overly fast Italian to condescendingly slow English, seemingly not caring just how much of it I understood. It was over an hour later before I was commanded back to my bed.

I had hoped the worst of it was over.

But no, the next day she ripped me from my bed, leading me down the hall and into a featureless cell. "You shall pray, and repent," she said, before slamming the door behind her.

STRANGE AND TWISTED THINGS

I do not think I am truly captive, I heard no lock at the door. But it is clear I can not leave. I am being offered no food, and being escorted straight back here after prayers. Usually, one of the girls comes to sit with me, smiling nastily, saying nothing when I try to speak with her.

Of course, I can not ask for the leaves. And I have nowhere to put the leeches that are expelled from my body. In fact, I must hide them. What would the nuns think, if such noxious creatures simply, magically appeared in a room where I am the only constant occupant?

I hate to think.

And so, they crawl over my body. They have migrated up to my bodice now, I can feel them under my arms, though I dare not look at them when anyone else is present, which is always. I hate this.

I am also being denied food, though they give me some bread every other day. They do not seek to outright kill me then. I almost wish they would.

August 3rd, 1847

Hunger gnaws at me, and the days drag by.

August 5th, 1847

I truly think I shall go mad here. I have begun to eat the leeches. I am hungry and there is nothing else to be done with them. It started when one fell from my skirts, I was so horrified that my chaperone might see it, and I could think of nothing else to do...

I can now see why witches made deals with devils. Where is my devil? Where is my hard bargain for my soul? I would take that Faustian bargain in a heartbeat. I yearn for it, I crave it. Worse than that, I am starting to think I need it. What else will save me?

August 6th, 1847

I hate this. Every day is torment and agony and nothing, nothing else. And I just have to sit here and wait. One day, I will have my own locked door. But I will have the key. And it will have wonderful things behind it, beautiful things. And I will have the key and no one, NO ONE apart from the people I allow will get inside. It will be nothing like this.

August 8th, 1847

I have taken to madly sketching the door, the one that will keep me safe. Over and over again, it is grand, and bright red (or it would be if I had the ink) with circles cut deep into the wood. It is mystery and power and beauty and safety and mine, mine, mine, mine.

I can think of nothing else.

August 9th, 1847

Sabina is here! Oh what a joy, what a joy!!! She has food for me, hidden under her skirts. I eat ravenously, not caring that I must look like a rabid animal as a tear into it with my teeth. She speaks, oh she speaks to me! I don't even care what about – although she has the most delightful news! She shall get her brother to inquire about me, to show the mother superior that I have people paying attention. That she can't just keep me here forever.

I didn't believe it at first. "But he will never do that!" I exclaimed. Why would he? We only met once.

"He will," she said with a smile. "He is my little brother. He wants me to be happy. Besides... he has asked me about you."

"He what?" I asked, my mouth still full of bread, how like a commoner I must have seemed.

"You made quite an impression on him," she teased. "And besides, he is a man. And he likes what he sees." I blush deeply, never expecting to get that kind of attention again.

But I would do anything to get out of this place. Anything.

August 10th, 1847

Sabina is back, she makes everything better. With a full belly, I have a clearer head. I can not stay here. And I can not wait to be saved. I will try and run. I need a few more days to get my strength back up, a few more solid meals. But then... I need to leave. Where? I have no idea. I need to go far, if anyone follows me, I will be easy to find, a crippled young lady with horrible Italian will not hide easily in the countryside. I must plan.

August 12th, 1847

Oh to be a man!! Finally I am out of that wretched room. I did not have to run after all. I heard Severino's voice in the courtyard and not an hour later, I was released. What happened? What did he say? Oh I am desperate to find out! But I can't ask him directly (of course) and I haven't had a chance to be alone with Sabina, not yet. All I can say now is, thank god for Severino. I owe him everything. I wonder when he will come and collect his due.

August 13th, 1847

More bad news, I'm afraid. I did not have the privacy to check my leg while I was in that horrible place, and I'm sad to say The Ugliness has spread. My skin is hardened and gray even above my hip now, the flesh there pockmarked and sagging as if I were an old man. An amputation at that point simply isn't possible. It has become me.

August 14th, 1847

I wanted to report something better, prettier. So I thought I'd let you know that I saw a dove today. I don't know where it came from, but it landed on the edge of the maze, peering down at me as I collected vegetables. The contrast of the green and white was so lovely. I'm glad I saw that.

August 15th, 1847

Severino came to see me. Gosh is that man handsome! Such dark eyes, such perfect features. And his hair! I just want to grab it, to pull him close and run my hands through it. It was all I could do not to throw myself at his feet in gratitude. I think he could tell, his smile was that of a man who was very pleased with himself. Very sure he would get what he wanted. Dare I flatter myself that maybe...he might want me?

"It didn't surprise me," he said, his voice rich and warm, heavy with an Italian accent that made my heart sing. "A lovely young lady like yourself should not be cooped up in a place like this. You are spirited. It is natural that you chafe at the rules."

I beamed at him. I didn't care that he looked me up and down as he spoke, eyeing me like a piece of meat. Truly I did not. To be entirely frank with you, if my body had not been covered in leeches, I would have torn my clothes off and thrown myself at him, right then and there. I wanted to. My blood runs hot now, I have forgotten how to be ashamed.

Instead he said, "But breaking into an office is...unusual. May I ask what you were looking for?"

I bit my lip, not sure how much I could share. "Well..." I started, leaning in a little closer to him. "I was curious. I wanted to know more about the history of this place. Mother Superior manages it so well after all." I said, blinking my eyes up at him, trying to look innocent.

He burst out laughing. "Alright then, don't tell me. I respect wanting to keep secrets, but if that really is what you want, you were looking in the wrong place."

"Oh?" I said, and something about the eagerness of my expression must have assured him of my sincerity.

"The monks have most of that information. History, philosophy, all that. The mother superior here... well, she's not so interested. Got too many spirited girls to keep in line, I think."

Ah! How his smile made me feel, and how this information made my heart dance. I don't know how it will help me, but at least it's a start.

August 17th, 1847

It's odd. I think Severino must truly like me. I don't think I've ever experienced that from a man before, well, not apart from Henry and my father.

He returned today, with news.

"I have arranged for one of the head monks to come over and give a talk." He announced, after sitting down and complimenting my hair.

"You said you were interested in history...how could I ignore such a noble desire?"

I gasped, my hand instinctively reaching out to grab his. "Have you? Have you really?" I asked, as he squeezed my hand. "But, the mother superior, she has to agree, and she keeps such a tight hold on everything."

He shrugged. "I presented it to her as a gift. 'Oh mother superior'" he said, imitating himself " I admire you so much, your dedication to bettering young women, thank you for taking care of my sister, etcetera, etcetera...' And I told her I went to the trouble of arranging a talk. In her honor. She simply couldn't say no"

I didn't hold myself back this time, I threw my arms around him and hugged him. Whatever price he asks, I will be happy to pay.

August 21st, 1847

I have thrown myself into my Italian studies. Whatever this monk has to say, I am determined to understand it. I think Sabina is tiring of me, slightly. She sighs every time I greet her in my horrible Italian, but she tries to put a brave face on it. Only a few more days, I want to tell her, but I can't. It's just that I must be able to understand what this man says, I must.

August 23rd, 1847

The monk comes tomorrow. I can scarcely breathe with anticipation, with hope. This could be everything, this has to be everything. It is the only path I can see forward, if this fails...I have nothing. If it succeeds, I could have my answer. My whole body trembled at the thought, at the black and white nature of what tomorrow will bring. Success, or failure, there are no other options.

Wish me luck.

August 24th, 1847

I am shaking so hard I can barely write. But I must, lest I forget what I heard.

The monk strode to the front of the room, brown robes swamping his small frame. He carried with him a heavy book, truly almost a tome. He slammed it down into the pulpit, a little burst of dust accompanying the loud sound.

"The history of this convent is an old and complex one," he said, his voice somewhat nasally, his throat hoarse. It would be difficult to listen to him under any other circumstances, but today I was enraptured.

"We've had some interest of late by men of science, come to look at the Roman ruins on which we are founded. While the pagans had been here since antiquity, it was only in 1156 that this order in particular was founded, and so..." Here I'm afraid I lost him, my Italian failing me. It was sometime before I could understand him again.

"Of course," He said "A maze is a misnomer. It is impossible to get lost inside the hedges. There is only one path, the point is simply to press forward. It is for contemplation, for slow repentance of our sins as we get closer to the center of all things – our lord and savior Jesus Christ. There was a time when the monks were expected to shuffle on their knees. This, of course, is not expected of you ladies." He laughed pitifully at his own joke.

"This is a reversal of how these things were once seen. These were once seen as an unavoidable descent into hell, or as traps, as with the minotaur in Greek antiquity. Thankfully we have moved on from this…In fact, there have been many attempts to remove the maze over the years, though it seems remarkably stubborn. Upon its planting, it was blessed by pope Adrian the fourth. It is said he buried some treasure there, either in the center or just outside of it, to ensure it would always be blessed by Christ…The pope at that point was… These days, of course, the vegetable garden is…the chapel was built in 1670…"

I was losing him, my head reeling with what he said. I heard him say something about a statue, in the center of the maze, or whatever it is.

Do I simply…go in? He certainly said something about it either being heaven, or hell. Either what you want to go towards, or what you want to escape. It had clearly been important, the pope did not bless every garden, and he certainly did not bury treasure very often. No, this seems older, somehow. If the pagans worshiped here, it must indeed be very old. Do I dare go up against that? Can I afford not to?

Once again a clear choice, no room for mediocrity, no room for a safe middle ground. All or nothing.

I feel a leech crawl up the back of my neck and I have decided – I'm going into the maze.

August 25th, 1847

I tried. I was so blinded by pain that at one point I was crawling on my knees. But I simply can not seem to get to the center, it's like there is always one more turn, one more twist of the pathway before I can finally get there. And besides, this leg slows me down so much. I am sure that if I could sprint, I could get there. I will try again tomorrow. I will try every day until I succeed.

September 1st, 1847

STRANGE AND TWISTED THINGS

I do not know where to begin, or what to do. My thoughts are a jumbled mess. Perhaps explaining it all will steady me.

First of all, as should come as no surprise to you, I was reckless and foolish. Severino had come to visit again, talking with his sister this time. I saw his horse, tied loosely just outside the convent gates, and…well, if sprinting was sure to get me in, a gallop could too, couldn't it?

I stole it. The man who has been so kind to me, who helped me unlocked this mystery…I stole from him. I walked quickly and with purpose, as if I was doing exactly as I should. I lead the hose, a beautiful chestnut creature, into the shadows, taking the long way around the convent walls, sneaking back in through a now disused servants' entrance. It seemed to take an age, I knew that if I were caught I would have no excuse whatsoever, and something told me Severino's kindness would not extend to excusing this. Somehow, I made it to the mouth of the maze uneducated.

I strapped myself to the horse, so that no matter what, as long as he kept moving, I would too. It was unbearable. I had expected him to hurry, but he was clearly not in the mood. The heat, I expect. He simply carried me forward, long after my body sagged and I could do nothing but collapse on top of him, focusing only on breathing. The pain was so intense I was sick, I'm loath to admit, all down the side of him. Still, he kept moving, far past the point where I would have been able to go. I believe I must have passed out at some point because the next thing I knew, we were in a large circle, a marble statue staring across from me.

And nine women all in white around me.

I practically rolled off the horse, trying to get a good look at them. But...they had no faces. I sank to my knees in shock. One came forward, lifting me up again with cold, dead hands.

"Hello..." I tried in Italian. They said nothing. I wondered if they could, without any mouths. Instead, it seemed to be the ground itself that spoke. In a language...it wasn't English. But it wasn't Italian either, I didn't have to struggle to understand. It was beyond language, it was if it were speaking in pure knowledge, in something older than human.

"Welcome, sister..." it said. It seemed to be a woman, though that was simply a ridiculous notion – how could the ground have a gender?

"We are pleased to see you. You are here for our help." She said both statements blandly, as if they were both equally under her control.

I let out a long, throaty sob. "Can you?" I asked, my desperation clear in my voice. "Help me?" My whole body was shaking by now.

"You have choices to make," she hissed. "But it is possible, yes."

"I'll do anything," I promised, and by God or the devil I meant it.

"Yes," she agreed simply. "Thankfully, what we ask is not too much."

"Did you do this to me? My leg. Did you...curse me?" I finally asked, wondering at last if I were speaking to friend or foe. Was this help, or was this blackmail?

"This is a difficult question," it said.

"How?" I barked back, perhaps a bit more aggressively than I had intended. It was just so hard to hold myself back, to not need....

"It is not clear where I begin, and where I end," she said simply, as if explaining things to a small child. "The right hand does not always know what the left is doing." She purred. "I cannot say I didn't do it. I cannot say I did."

I just stared at the statue, deciding that was as good a thing as any to address. I wanted to focus on something, bring the voice just slightly more into the corporeal world.

"What does that even mean?" I asked, my mouth hanging open slightly.

"I am many things. But I am not...human," it said, as if it weren't sure that was quite the right word for me. "We lack physicality."

I found, suddenly, I didn't care. I just wanted it to be over. Perhaps one day I will regret that. But now, I long only for this to be finally finished.

"Tell me what to do."

"The Pope. As you know he buried something here. It is... distasteful to us. It is what makes the maze so difficult for you to enter. It is what makes it impossible for us to leave. I want it removed. It should be no trouble for you."

I don't care. I didn't care then, and I don't care now, what ramifications it would lead to, releasing this thing into the world. My logic was simple, if it could affect me all the way over in England, surely it was not that well-contained in the first place.

Perhaps I should have considered it longer. I know I am weak. I know this place's great risk to others. But I cannot be expected to bear the weight of evil alone. I refuse. Besides, I had a plan.

I dug up the whole area, working late into the night. The moon, almost full once more, aiding my work. Occasionally I glanced at the girls in white. They stood perfectly still, not one of them moving an inch, simply watching me with mounting interest. Perhaps it was my imagination, but it felt like they were excited for me. Finally, I found it, my shovel hitting hard silver.

"Yes..." The garden hummed around me. "Yes..."

I pulled it out, throwing it open. In it...everything you'd expect. A bible. Rosary. A vial of blood. A bone, presumably of one saint or another. A ring stamped with the papal seal.

"Get it out. Get it far away from here," the statue told me, her voice excited and high.

"You said you'd help me," I countered, struggling to my feet.

"And so shall I. Once you get that out of here, it will be easy for you to return. And besides, I need a lamb to do my work. Fetch me one, and all you desire shall become yours."

I flew. I hurled myself back on the horse and forced him onward, working him up into a trot he clearly did not want. I did not care. Together, we rode towards a local farm I had seen on my way here.

It was dingy and dark there, but that hardly mattered. I grabbed a lamb, soft and fluffy in my hands. I rode back, slowly and quietly this time, but heart hammering. It was almost dawn by the time we were back.

She was right, it was easy to re-enter this time. So much in fact, that I marvelled it had ever taken any trouble at all.

In no time at all, I stood in front of the statue, gazing up at it in wonder. I hadn't taken the time to really admire her before, but now I felt I couldn't keep my eyes off of her. She was stunningly gorgeous, with a mountain of shells at her feet and a massive sword at her side. Her breasts were plump and heavy, she seemed unashamed of her nakedness. I liked that.

And then she began to move, slowly, mesmerizingly. No sudden movements but instead a constant flow, one that was utterly foreign to the marble it was made of.

"We thank you," she said again.

"My leg," I was too tired to be polite, too afraid.

"Of course. Remove your fake one and place the lamb before me."

It bleated softly in my arms, nuzzling its face into me.

"Will you hurt it?" I asked.

"Yes," it said simply.

I swallowed. But still I held my chin high. I had eaten meat before, and I would again. I had wasted meat even, taking more than my share and leaving it to rot. This was no different, and how dare you judge me for it, diary? I did as she asked, sitting on the floor in front of the statue.

She...molded it. Like wax halfway hard, she crushed and formed it, smoothing out certain parts, elongating others. She twisted the fur back into its skin, working it into the finest white flesh. And then she poured it towards me, in a way I simply cannot fathom. It slithered up my skirt, grazing my stump of a leg. And then it *was* my leg. I could feel it, I could kick it. I could move it!

I threw my head back and laughed and laughed. I had never felt so good! I felt...pure. As if my soul had just been washed, something deep and hidden inside me now suddenly gone. I stayed there for a long time.

"The leeches – " I started.

"Are gone and will stay that way," she assured me. "Your other leg too, should be better."

I gasped, pulling up my skirts. *Yes! Yes!* My skin was soft and pale, flawless as before! Not a hint of The Ugliness, not a touch of gray! I swear I even smelled better!

"Thank you, thank you," I repeated over and over, my body shaking with joy. I was whole, I was well, I was pure. I was beautiful. I am me again.

In time, I was able to get up. What a strange sensation, after all this time! My own two feet! I couldn't help it, I jumped, danced and skipped all around the circle.

Finally, as the sun peeked into the sky, the first pink tendrils of dawn blessing the night, I took my leave. But she wasn't done yet.

"We know you still have the box," she said, just as I was about to turn the first corner. I felt my face go white. "You did not leave it at the farm. We trust you will use it wisely. You have seen our power."

"I – I don't know what to do with it." I started lying. I had wanted the protection, wanted to keep it just in case.

But it would say no more.

September 3rd, 1847

I find I am waiting for the apocalypse. What was that thing I unleashed? Some ancient evil, simply waiting, biding its time, for a stupid girl to fall victim to her own vanity and unleash it? Some devil, old as the bible, using its cunning and manipulation to trick me into doing its bidding?

But no. Not yet at least. The weather is unseasonably fair, the last breath of summer blowing over our fields and down the coast. The birds still sing, the flowers are still sweet. I am...happy. There seems to be peace here. Nothing of note has happened, nothing at all. Well, apart from the fact that Severino had a fit when he found out his horse was missing. Blamed the sisters for not looking after it properly. Apparently he called the Mother Superior a "useless old hag." Gosh, how I wish I had been there to see her face when he said that! Still. I was able to return it. I set it free around the edge of the convent, confident it would wander back to him. It did, and all is well there too.

I have not told anyone about my leg. I don't know what to do. How do I even say it? "Oh, look, I have another leg now! What a surprise!" It's not like I can show people it slowly growing in. It simply wasn't there one day and it was the next. I have to admit, I hadn't considered this issue when I took the garden up on her offer. Besides,

September 5th, 1847

I must apologize, I was interrupted while writing to you last. Sister Mary Emilia had fallen, clattering down the stairs with a giant crash.

I was, of course, terrified for her, jabbering away in Italian that felt smooth at the time, but now I'm certain was wrong. What happened? Is it The Ugliness again? The same fate that befell me?

The others think I am mad. I burst into tears when I saw her on the ground, despite the fact that at most, she had sprained an ankle. I was just so afraid that I had merely passed on my affliction, and not ended it. I couldn't say that to them, of course, and had no excuse at all, making me seem even more insane. Oh hell! I meant what I wrote yesterday, about not being sorry. But I mean this too. I am most dreadfully and utterly worried. I feel both within me most profoundly. I will have to think carefully about what to do.

I will keep a very close eye on her. I feel even more afraid for her than I did for myself, a feat I didn't know I was capable of. May fate have mercy on her.

As for me, I still walk around with my wooden leg, my real one bent up above it. It hurts more than I can tell you, my knee rubbed raw and bleeding most days. But still. How on earth can I explain that it has grown back? Surely they will accuse me of witchcraft or devilry.

Besides, I don't know what I want to do yet. Even with a fully healed body, can I return home, to England? Whereas once the idea would have filled me with wild hope, now I am... a little more cautious. I have no true friends there. Even my own mother seemed happy to see the back of me.

I miss Father and Henry desperately, of course. But if I go, it will set the course for my entire life. And besides, with the annulled marriage...and time spent in Italy... how would that look to a potential suitor? Would my former 'husband' still be my best option? Perhaps. Perhaps not. The truth is, I have no idea what awaits me there. And that fact alone is enough to make me cautious.

I could run. With two legs and slightly better Italian, I think my chances in a city here are fair. I could tutor children in English perhaps, be a governess, although without references or introductions, this would prove challenging. But not impossible.

Or I could stay, keep an eye on the maze. Flirt with Severino. Gossip with Sabina. I am shocked to find this doesn't seem like my worst option, and part of me wishes I could choose it. But I did not go through everything I have done to be simply locked up in a convent. I did not sacrifice that poor lamb just so its flesh could lie, mangled and useless, beneath my skirts as if it had never happened at all.

I intend to dance. And run, and ride, and play. I am almost overwhelmed with memories of how good that was. To simply be carefree. To not know or even care what evils plagues this world. It was foolish of me, and shallow, yes. But it was bliss.

But how? And after that, what?

September 7th, 1847

I feel sick with worry. It is so much worse, to see the dark fruits of your labor spread bare before you. Every time Sister Maria Emila so much as sighs, I am next to her, carrying her things or fetching her water. I obsessively ask how she sleeps. She says she is fine, but I don't know. I mean, I certainly didn't tell anyone when I was in her condition, not until I absolutely had to. And even then it was my mother, not some random convent girl I hardly knew. I wish there was some way to gain her trust, to figure this out, but honestly I can't see a way forward, not without admitting my own affliction. And I would rather die than do that. It shocks me to say it, but I would rather see her die too.

I am sorry about that. But I am certain of it.

All I can do for now is wait.

September 8th, 1847

Well! It seems I have thoroughly annoyed Sister Maria Emila with my concern. I have been by her side all these last few days, constantly asking after her health, dropping hints about how I knew what it was like to have an 'issue' with one's leg. She didn't seem to pick up on this at all, and is now happily walking around. Finally she snapped at me: "I have prayed to God, he has listened, I am healed. Now will you please leave me be?" And she practically ran off! Both legs clearly working perfectly!!

God, I'm so relieved I could cry. I feel a singing in my chest, a joy in my bones. Everyone is commenting on it, some teasing me that I must have a secret lover. Some wildly disapproving. But I just can't seem to care. I am happy. All is well.

But it is, perhaps, an overreaction. This whole thing has been. I can't react like this every time someone has a fall. People fall for reasons not related to my ugliness. I have to calm down.

September 12th, 1847

I don't know why, but I visited the maze again this morning. I guess it was nice to walk through it calmly, without fear of pain or suffering. It was a lovely experience; I can see why some people would enjoy it. You don't have to do anything other than put one foot in front of the other, you are guided perfectly. And yet, you have complete freedom and privacy to contemplate your own thoughts. I spoke to the garden. She didn't speak back, although I'm not sure if I really expected her to. It would have been strange, I think, for her to speak during the day. I don't know why I think this, but I do.

Still, I think I shall visit again, I feel called, somehow, to that place. As if it is part of me, and I am part of it. That is something I must take into account. If I leave the convent, I will leave the garden, and I'm not sure I can bear that. It is the only thing that has ever truly helped me.

September 13th, 1847

I am surprised at how little guilt I feel. Perhaps I am evil. At this moment, I am only grateful my suffering is over.

September 14th, 1847

And yet, this has been going on too long. I have two legs and I am determined to use them. The time has come to make a choice, I refuse to simply cower in indecision. This convent cannot be my whole world, it cannot be the only walls I ever know for the rest of my life. Or if it is, it will be my choice. One that I choose freely and joyfully. I will give myself three more days, and then, I will have picked my path, for better or worse.

Severino visited again today. I must have imagined it, but he seemed less enamored with me today. Disappointed, even, to see me. God, men are so fickle! Why did I pin so much hope in him? I suppose I thought, now that I did not have to conceal the leeches...but no, frankly I blush even to write it. Besides, he never knew about them, and so he cannot possibly know about the change, know I am ready to...well! You know what I mean. Although, after all I have been through, all I have done, I see no earthly reason why the marriage bed is what I should be ashamed of. My body is truly a gift, a gift from some supernatural being. I think, one day, I will find the right person to share it with. But for now, nothing keeps me here. Nothing apart from the maze, and I shall find some way to visit that. I have solved trickier puzzles by now, after all.

September 15th, 1847

I decided to consult the maze once again. It calls to me. I ache to be there. I feel safe there, I feel whole. I feel as if my choices actually matter, as if who I am matters. I went at night this time, hoping for answers. I found that there was another faceless girl there, all in white. The tenth, whereas before there had been nine.

"Is this..." I couldn't help but ask, gesturing at the girl. I wasn't actually sure if the garden could see, having no eyes. But presumably she did, because she said –

"An innocent soul, harvested and corrupted by me? Yes," the garden intoned, in the same calm voice, as if it were commenting on the weather.

I stared at the new girl for some time. There was nothing distinctive about her, nothing to set her apart from the others, just that she seemed fresher somehow. Her glow was a little brighter, her movements slightly more awkward. Beyond that I can't truly describe it. She was simply newer than the others.

I sat down before her, removing my fake leg with a sigh, allowing my real one to stretch out before me. As always, it felt glorious. And yet, I could not find comfort. The ground was hard and cold, I struggled to find a clear spot amongst the roots that popped out from the earth. But still. It was peaceful there. I was not afraid, although I had some sort of abstract idea that I should be.

"Why?" I asked simply, not knowing myself exactly what I was asking, but trusting that she would know, somehow.

I was surprised to find that instead of being mysterious and vague, the garden poured out its secrets. It had no shame. It explained to me that it didn't want to punish humans necessary, but it would one day destroy them. Perhaps it's because it said it in such a calm manner that I was not utterly horrified. Destroy humanity? Surely not all of it? How? That was so big, so important it seemed impossible to gasp somehow. But then I thought of my family wasting away, as I had, my home crumbling to dust. Henry in a coffin, Sabina being ripped apart by some ancient force. That made me cry. Yes. That is what truly affected me, not the thought of the millions of people I had never met dying and suffering. That left me cold and unaffected. I am sorry, and I hope most people are better than me. But my tears fell for Henry, and only a very few others.

"Much has to pass before that will happen," she said gently. "Many years. At least a hundred, before the discord and plague even begins."

I swallowed hard. Was that really so bad? It is, of course it is. I must remind myself of that. Worldwide chaos and destruction is truly evil. But...at least I won't live to see it. And neither will my family, or anyone I have ever known. And I don't really care, even if it is my fault. I know that is selfish. I don't know what else to say.

"But now. These days. You...torment people. People like me. Surely you could have just asked me to come, to remove the box...What I went through...It was the worst thing I can imagine. It was unrelenting hell on earth," I said, my voice cracking. "I would have come, if you had just asked. Why didn't you?"

Again, the answer was clear and uncomplicated

"I like to play. I like to see them twist and turn, to witness their desperation and prayers. I have little other entertainment." Somehow, I could hear that she was smiling.

"Are you playing now?" I asked, my mouth suddenly dry. I should bring wine next time.

"There is a boy in Athens I have my eye on. He is about to drown himself, over a girl he only ever imagined. A few in the Americas. One old German man – I think he will go mad, mad enough to harm his whole family. Probably kill them, and only understand what he is doing as the light leaves their eyes. He has already started his slow descent. It is beautiful, if you have the right perspective." I couldn't even imagine it. What chaos, what pain she was wreaking throughout the world.

"What happens if I bring the box back?" I ask. I wondered if it was a stupid question, if she would lash out at me, curse me again. But then, she seemed to know everything else, every thought I had so... why not ask? Still, I began to nervously rip up a leaf that had fallen beside me, its veins coming apart in my hands.

"My powers would be severely curtailed once more. And I would only be able to focus my energies on playing with one person at a time," she explained, almost kindly.

"And that would be...me?" I asked, my voice small.

"That is a reasonable assumption," she said, and we lapsed into silence. It surprised me when she spoke again, she had only ever replied to my questions before then.

"Whatever you decide, I want you to know that you have done better than almost any human I have ever met. You have endured much. I am sorry you have no one to share that with. You should be proud."

"Thank you," I whispered, looking up at the stars above. They twinkled merrily down at me, a cool breeze suddenly lifting my hair. And I knew she had done it. I was never going to return the box.

Chapter Sixteen

Greta was just glad that this time, she wasn't wearing her wedding dress. She invited her nephew in with a small nod, laying out tea and biscuits for them both. Though he was obviously and clearly an adult, she could have sworn he had grown since the last time she saw him. Or perhaps she had just shrunk. Either way, he was a bear of a man, with huge hulking shoulders and a great, fluffy beard. There was nothing subtle about him.

It had been eleven days since anyone had heard from Mark – well, apart from his voice inside the book, of course. But she hardly felt that counted. Her days had been nice and predictable, better, in fact, now her brother was gone. She had one less thing to worry about, simply keeping to her routine of checking the mail, cleaning and feeding, watching her beautiful dancers. She hadn't cried once over him.

Greta and Nicco simply exchanged pleasantries at first. No one could fail to see how sick she was now, how oddly she moved. He was polite enough to wish her well. But it didn't take him long to dive right into it.

"Look," he said, scratching behind his ear. "My dad...no one has seen him in a while."

"I know dear," she said, trying to sound sad. It was a struggle. "But I'm sure he will show up. He's always had a temper, ever since he was a child. He just needs to cool down I think." She tried to sound confident. Really, she just seemed a bit heartless.

"Well," he said, setting his tea down. "I'm not so sure."

"Oh?" she asked, taking a long sip herself.

"I...well. I know he came to visit you, that night."

"Yes," she said evenly. She held his gaze, refusing to make this easy on him. He looked away, blushing. If he was going to accuse her of anything, he would have to do it right to her face.

"Well... no one knows where he went after that," he mumbled into his cup.

"Don't they?" she asked. "I assumed he went home. I didn't ask. We weren't on good terms, not since he paid people to break into my house." She didn't bother hiding the venom in her voice.

Here, he had the good grace to wince. "I know. But if you could help us find him, we'd appreciate it..."

"Who is the 'we' here? As far as I know, you and I are his only living relatives," she remarked casually. Plus, he didn't have any friends, although she had the good grace not to point this out.

"My wife and I. She's pregnant with our second child. He was going to help us out a bit, you know, babysit and all that."

So like that side of the family, she thought bitterly. Only looking for his father so the man can do something for him. It was almost pathetic how needy they were, how much they always took from others. She would never do that. Still, she didn't know his wife was pregnant again, and for that she felt guilty. They were still family, after all.

"Congratulations on the new baby," she said stiffly.

"Thank you. But...I'm afraid I still have some questions for you. My father...isn't the first person to go missing after coming here, is he?" This time he didn't flinch, didn't break eye contact with her. His look was firm and unyielding.

"And I was wondering if you knew anything about that. Or perhaps the rumors that have been flying about? Rumors about curses, ghosts. About strange women who seem to like frightening people." He was clearly trying to keep his temper under control.

She let out a tight, high laugh. "You can't believe that," she said, fear making her voice shrill. "All that nonsense about ghosts! That's madness, a fairy tale, an urban legend. And quite frankly – "

"I don't know what to believe," he retorted. "But I do believe that no one has asked you any difficult questions. Not about that poor boy that went missing, or the one that almost broke his neck, or your 'friend' that fell down the stairs, or my dad. And I rather think that's an issue, don't you?" He was practically snarling at her, gathering momentum with each word that passed. Just like his father.

"I, I don't know what – " She started, mouth suddenly dry. How she wished he had visited later in the day, when the night was close and the shadows strong. Instead, sunlight streamed in, almost painfully bright.

"Don't play the innocent old woman with me," he barked.

"Don't yell at me in my own home," she shot back, suddenly just as furious as he was. How dare another useless man come into her own home and accuse her? With no evidence, no understanding at all of what she'd done, who she was.

"You've always hated my father, always wanted what he had."

At this last accusation, she screamed in indignation, throwing her hands up in the air. "He had *nothing* to want. Nothing. He was useless, spoiled, jealous. He never grew up, he was a horrible, vile little man. He was a parasite." With this she was on her feet, fuming.

"Was," he said, suddenly quiet. "You know exactly what happened to him. Don't you?"

For a moment, there was stillness, neither moving or breathing. Then he launched himself at her, pushing her to the floor, the tea-set going flying, spending scalding water everywhere. Her head smashed against the marble fireplace, so hard her vision went black. Then he was on top of her, fist raised.

She didn't even hesitate, she grabbed the diary, so precious to her, and clung to it, no thought for her own fate. She couldn't risk it getting wet, couldn't bear the idea of the precious ink running. But that was a mistake too.

Not knowing anything more than how important it must be, he grabbed it, literally clawing it from her arms, assuming it to be valuable just because she wanted it. For a moment they tousled over it, her gnarled hands surprisingly strong, for once thankful for their unrelenting stiffness.

It ripped in half, she with the beginning and he with the end, the middle pages flying across the room, scattered like rose petals. And then the strangest thing happened. Somehow, it didn't feel like it was just her screaming, it felt like the whole house was, around her and inside her, just howling with rage and pain.

It must have been loud, because before she knew it, there was a knock at the front door.

"Are you alright?" someone called through the letterbox. "Have you fallen? Do you need an ambulance?" Their voice was muffled, almost impossible to hear over the din inside. But hear it he did. Knowing that he had little other than a flimsy accusation, and having clearly attacked an old lady, Nicco fled. Out the back door and down the stairs, carrying his precious pages with him.

She gulped, hard, knowing exactly what he would find if he read that book. She had read it back to back, cover to cover, so many times by now, she could almost recreate it from memory. And so she knew exactly how dangerous it was, knew that within those pages was the key to destroying the house – and whatever lived inside of it – once and for all.

She raced after him as best as she could, hobbling down the back stairs and fumbling her way into her car. That was his main mistake, on foot she would never be able to catch him, but driving she at least had a chance. She sped after him, no plan in place, no next move in mind, nothing apart from the need to retrieve that diary.

She flew onto the main road, the Tuscan forests rising up on either side of the thin pathway. In truth she hated these roads, always had. They were narrow and twisted, the people that drove down them often drunk or simply crazy. You had to be confident to navigate them, it was so easy to miss a turn, to be swept off, suddenly far away from where you needed to be, the road too narrow to let you turn around.

But she couldn't afford to let that stop her. She was propelled by pain. Everything hurt. As it always had, as it had every single moment, of every single day since Fredeick had left. It had been there for so long, she had almost, almost been able to forget about it. But now it was all she felt, despair gripping at her throat, her lungs. She couldn't face more loss, couldn't let go of that book.

So when she finally saw her nephew's car, finally sped up behind it, she didn't hesitate. She rammed him from behind, slamming her car into his, trying desperately to get him off the road. Nothing else mattered.

He was clearly not ready for this, no matter how much he claimed he knew. She was close enough to see his face now, white as a sheet and wide-eyed. He hadn't actually believed it, she realized now, with something akin to disdain rising up inside her. He didn't believe that she was actually capable of those horrible things -- she could see it, the shock, the horror of the realization, written across his face.

But he didn't stop. Instead he floored it, accelerating as hard and as fast as he could.

She smiled. She was suddenly free, free to do whatever she liked. She had been holding it together for so long, happy to be the little old lady who stood by the sidelines, who cheered people on. That wasn't her anymore.

She stayed close, suddenly finding reckless driving to be easy, some supernatural power guiding her, or perhaps it was her own insane confidence. But as he turned, wheels skidding as he made a sudden left turn, she followed suit, not caring that two wheels actually left the ground as she did so. Her heart beat wildly, her palms sweaty, but her driving never faltered. She laid on the horn instead, she didn't know why, to scare him probably, or just to express her own rage.

He jumped, she could see it, his shoulders tense, neck covered in sweat. He jerked the steering wheel again, this time heading down a narrow dirt path, so tiny she hadn't even noticed it before. Still, she kept going, following without hesitation. The car now bumping up and down over tree roots, her body moving with it.

He must know these roads well, she reflected, wondering what on earth would bring a man like that out to such a remote place. She hated to think.

But then – yet another turn, this time almost a full ninety degrees as he swung the car around. It was her time to scream now. She was too late. She hit a tree at full force, hearing the trunk crunch against her car, feeling the airbag leap out and into her chest. Pain like she had never felt before crashing over her, radiating through every cell in her body.

And all was still.

For one long moment, she simply sat there, frozen, unable to comprehend what had just happened. Slowly it dawned on her, accepting it without comment. She grappled with her seat belt, staggering out of her car just in time to hear the last of Nicco's motor, speeding away. She felt her shoulders sag, all fight now out of her. But she couldn't let him go. Couldn't just let him win.

She had no idea how she got home. She must have been in a daze, it wouldn't have surprised her if she had suffered a concussion. But eventually, she returned, just as night was falling, and the clouds made way for the moon.

She had never been so happy to see her house, resolving never to leave it again. Of course, that was if she didn't get arrested. She winced, thinking about the trail of evidence she must have left behind. Any number of people could have seen her, she had hardly been subtle. And when one car rammed another, there were clues, weren't there? Paint chips and things? And that's if Nicco didn't have a camera in his car – people do these days, don't they? Not to mention her own car, left behind, smashed into a tree. Surely that alone was evidence enough.

But she found she just didn't care. It had been electric. She had felt alive. So much more than she had ever felt before, like she was powerful, like she could do things. Like she mattered.

So when she finally appeared at the house, she wasn't tired at all, but energized, committed to doing anything she could to stop Nicco. Because he was coming alright, she had no doubt about that. He was not a kind man, and revenge would be the top thing in his mind. He wanted to destroy her, and her home. With the book in his possession, he would know exactly how.

Chapter Seventeen

September 16th, 1847

I think I want to go to America. I have heard that people can make their fortunes there, and there are so many immigrants, one lone English woman should not be too out of place. Besides, I have heard that members of the fairer sex are allowed to serve as nurses, because of their civil war. I find that blood and death do not scare me these days. Even a year ago this would have seemed like a ludicrously audacious plan. But now...it seems so much easier than what I have already been through. And I do want to help. I do have compassion, some of it at least.

I keep thinking about that poor German man. Wondering if he has hurt his family yet – and if he knows what fate has in store for him. Still, I will not return the box, though I still have it.

Bad things happen, it can't all be laid at my doorstep.

September 18th, 1847

It worked! It actually worked, my plan! (Not America, something else!) I want to sing!

September 20th, 1847

I must apologize for writing so little. I was simply so overcome with joy and, I must admit, pride. Sinful, arrogant, wicked pride. I have done it. I feel as if I have won, tricked everyone.

It was something Sister Maria Emila said, "I prayed to god and he healed me." I should have seen it sooner. How did I not?!

That evening, just before our prayers, I removed my wooden leg. I approached the chapel as calmly as I could, though I felt sure I was about to faint from fear. I was so worried people would notice how well I was walking, would comment on the lack of sound – that horrible, nasty thudding it always used to make. But they didn't! No one noticed! Ah, being ignored can have its perks, I see now.

About halfway through the service, I threw myself down on the ground. The nuns gasped and yelled, running from me as if I were possessed. I can't blame them. I began to yell, "God almighty, I feel your love!" I cried out. "Mother Mary, I see you! I see you!" Pointing up to the cross. My whole body was shaking now, almost too afraid to go on. But I was committed. "The light! The light!" I called out. "The light of God is upon me."

And I kicked my leg out from under my skirts. The nuns screamed, total chaos reigning, some trying to help me, others trying to leave.

I simply couldn't hold it in anymore. I burst into laughter. "It's a miracle!" I called out through my giggles, before nattering on a bit more about God and his divine mercy.

Clearly assuming I was overcome by divine light, they led me away, giving me some strong brandy. The whole convent descended into total chaos! People were screaming, crying, falling to their knees and praising God! Oh, I wish you could have seen the mayhem, it was so.... Electric! Alive! But for now, I must go. I will write more soon, at the moment people are constantly buzzing around me, wanting to talk about it. "How did it feel?" "What did you see?" "Can I touch your leg?" "Do you feel different now?" So many questions! I shall make up wonderful and scandalous answers to all of them. Ah! I love it!

September 21st, 1847

The deception has taken off far more than I could possibly have imagined! The people of the nearby villages have come to pray with me, as if my 'good fortune' could rub off on them. People are enthralled, they want me to give talks and speeches. I do believe I am a little bit famous! I mentioned wanting to become a nurse and people practically keeled over with joy, insisting I must have healing hands now. Someone even suggested a lecture tour! I must ask the garden if she has anything she wants me to say, any message to impart. I owe her everything.

Mother Superior is deeply suspicious, but then I can't blame her. I haven't exactly been pious and so this miracle cure is hardly logical. But she can't say anything, everyone else is so wrapped up in the idea. Besides, who is she to question God, ha! Submit, ye wicked woman! I think she may even be a little jealous. In all her long, miserable life, God has never so much as whispered in her ear, let alone performed a miracle.

And it's because of her that this has all worked out so well, for she and four other reliable witnesses can all attest to examining me thoroughly when I first arrived. Oh, how I hated that then, being probed and prodded, and how grateful I am for it now! They can all confirm that when I arrived, I had only one leg, and now, well, clearly.... it must truly be a divine gift from God!

I want to tell the garden all about it. I know she probably already knows, but I have no one else to tell. Sabina laps it up, obviously. She is very proud to have a friend who is a "favorite of god" as she puts it. She keeps 'tending to me' and shooing away the other nuns so I can 'rest', while we all know she just wants to gossip. I love her.

September 23rd, 1847

And yet, I am almost fully packed. I will be leaving, obviously. This is no place for me. There is not enough joy, enough life. But still…I will miss her, profoundly. I promise to write, and she promises to write back, but we know it will not be the same. I never thought I'd be sad to leave this place.

September 24th, 1847

I am giddy, my good fortune coming in wave after wave. Severino came to see me. To congratulate me, of course. He was most happy to hear my news, even wanting to see the evidence for himself. I shan't go into details, that is not lady like. But I did show him. And we made love.

An unmarried woman in the house of God, with a man she wasn't even promised to. It was wild, and it was sweet, and I now know why people get married. To my sins, my vanity, pride and sloth, you may now add lust.

But then he spoke

"I know you went into the maze." He said, watching me arrange my skirts. I froze, my skin suddenly cold.

"No one will believe you." I said, recalling the mountains of praise I have already had. The nuns could all confirm my story. But he was a man, after all. Would that have more sway? Probably. He was rich too, and well connected. That might be enough, easily could be, in fact. I was angry in that moment, more angry than I could possibly tell you. I wanted to run back to the maze, beg to be remade yet again – as a man this time. As anything fierce and powerful, anything unafraid. In that second, I hated him.

But his words cooled my anger at once. "As if I would tell anyone," he said, gently taking my hand.

I simply stared at him, for once lost for words.

"I respect those who take what they want. You are as bold as you are beautiful." And with this, he kissed my knuckles, a gesture somehow even more intimate than what we had done before.

"How..." I asked, hardly sure where to begin. How could he tell? How had he known the maze was powerful? How long had he known? Finally I choked out: "How...dare you say this to me now...after we just..?"

"Of course I say it afterwards" His voice was low and sultry. "I wanted you. Why risk saying it before? It could have ruined everything."

"It would have made no difference..." I muttered, shocked at the truth in my own words.

He smiled mysteriously, almost a smirk. "This land is old. It has made pacts before. My family is... no stranger to these deals. Though I think you may have gone further than even we dared." But there was no admonishment in his eyes, only affection. I blushed, looking down at our entwined fingers. I couldn't deny it. I didn't want to.

"That's why you had the monk come and give a talk. You were helping me," I realized, a girlish bubble of admiration jumping to my heart.

"I couldn't be sure exactly who you were, or what you wanted. But I thought I would do my best to help, yes," he explained. "I hoped, I suppose, that the maze would call someone like you next. Someone...delectable."

I blushed, somehow, after all this, still clinging to some shred of priority. He laughed joyously, pulling me even closer.

"But yes. I have always hoped it was you," he said, looking deep into my eyes.

"That's why you looked so sad the last time I saw you. Before I debuted my new leg. You thought I had failed, rejected her offer." I stared at him in bewilderment.

He nodded, kissing the top of my head. "I should never have doubted you," he practically purred at me, looking at me long and hard. I couldn't help it, so I kissed him again.

And then suddenly he pulled back, cupping my face in his hands. "I want you as my wife." He said, though he had already had his spoils.

I tell you in truth, dear diary, I had never dreamed of this. Marriage and its pleasures had been so far away from my mind for so long, I thought that door closed to me forever. How happy I am to be wrong in this.

I threw my arms around him, almost knocking him backwards. We laughed and giggled and made love once more. We put on quite a show. I hope God was watching, I want Him to know that we won.

And so, I am to become Violetta Ricci, wife to one of the most prominent noble families in Italy. I have no words to express my joy.

January 26th, 1848

I know I have not written in some time, but things have been going so well, and to be honest I find you such a painful reminder of worse times... times I would rather forget.

But I thought you might like to know that I am wed. It was truly a triumph. Henry came, all the way from England, as did my father. Oh, what a joy it was to see them. My heart...I feel so radiantly happy. I cannot begin to describe the joy one finds with true family, especially when you never thought to be reunited again. And on such an occasion! Mother did not come, obviously. I did not expect it. I did, however, send her a marvelous portrait of myself and my new husband. I fully admit that it was to spite her, show her who I could become without her. I hope she is jealous. I hope it hurts.

My gown was superb, in the absolute latest fashion, of course. Folds of white silk (again, for our queen, I may be fluent in Italian now but I am still English), mountains of lace, diamonds at my ears, pearls at my neck. White roses everywhere one looked, perfuming the air with a divine sweetness.

But even better, no lecherous men. No leeches, no fire, no fear. It was perfect.

Sabina is now my sister, and a better sister I could never have dreamed of. Of course, she too knew about the maze the whole time. She too had high hopes for me. How profoundly I adore that woman. I live not too far away from the convent now, a short ride in my new carriage, even less on one of the many fine horses Severino has given me. Even my mother-in-law is not fully distasteful, though she is a passionate woman that rules the men in her household with an iron fist. Severino insists that I will come to like her in time, and I have determined to try my best.

You may have noticed that my dreams of going to America and becoming a nurse have vanished. Oh diary, I know. I know I am wicked. I should go and help people. But I am so, so happy. It is as if someone is massaging sunlight into my soul. Every day I do not wake up in that hell is a blessing. The novelty has not worn off yet. I hope it never shall.

My life is better than I ever could have dreamed. Even before The Ugliness started, I dreamed I would be rich and beautiful. I never dared to dream that I would be happy. That my husband would actually love me.

He listens to me. He talks to me, really talks, as if to an equal. He seems to truly know me, anticipating my needs, bringing me presents and delights that even I didn't know I wanted. Every day we laugh together, like school children, just...happy.

That isn't to say that we don't fight. We do. I have broken more vases than I can count, hurling them at walls and screeching like the devil. I am unyielding and demanding when I know I am right. But I love it, and I think somehow he understands this. I love hearing my own voice, I love demanding what I'm due, I love telling people exactly what I think. He never asks me to do anything less.

Almost always, we make love after. He devours me, and I devour him back, the passion we share almost enough to bring me to tears, were it not so infinitely good.

I do insist that we support the poor, and I actually follow through on that. Since I have joined the family, we have been giving far more to those in need – and less to the church. You would think fear or guilt would compel me to enrich their coffers, but it simply does not. I don't trust what I can't see. I can see how much happier the villages are now, how many dowries we have been able to supply, how many educations advanced. No one here goes hungry.

It is interesting. The maze seems to be an open secret among my new family. Sabina visits it often while she lives at the convent, and sends back leaves for her mother. I know not what she does with them, she never seems to be in any physical pain. I do not feel I can ask, or even that I want to. They have never questioned why their eldest son married a disgraced and effectively penniless girl from England, and I am more grateful for this kindness than I can say.

Strangely, Sabina says the convent has been getting...worse. The mother superior has come down with a hacking cough, some sort of illness the doctors can't figure out. There are enough of those going around, to be sure, it is possible she simply has been near too many bad smells. But it is also possible she has been picked to 'play in the garden' as I once heard my mother-in-law so eloquently put it. Although I must say, it typically prefers prettier women. But I can't discount the possibility entirely.

Especially since misfortune seems to be befalling the very convent itself. Apparently part of the roof collapsed during a bad storm, and there was a small fire in the kitchens.

These things do happen of course. But I can't help but wonder...would they have happened, if I had acted differently?

February 15th, 1848

I destroyed the box yesterday. I sold the Bible, its age giving it some value. I poured the blood, still fresh and fluid, into the ocean. I smashed the bone against the rocks. I burned the rosary, the slender cord sizzling in the heat, the beads rolling out onto the marble fireplace.

No hellfire rained down on me, no angry God smote me down.

I wonder about that often. Why was it so easy for the garden to talk to me? Why does God refuse me? I have not forgotten what she said, that she would one day destroy all humanity. I know, and I feel I must apologize to you, dear diary, for you shall surely survive far longer than I. Perhaps you will see darkness even I can not dream of.

But the garden was there for me. She was real. When I was at my lowest, she pulled me up again. Her and Severino are the only ones to have ever done that for me, and for this they have my loyalty. I am sorry. Ask God why he is not kinder.

February 20th, 1848

Perhaps God finally has risen up and defended 'his people' after all. I feel sick, sick with fear and confusion. There was yet another fire at the convent. (I swear, this cannot all be coincidence. I know the maze is at work- but did she go too far this time?) But this one seemed to be different. It spread through the garden, the flame not orange but blue, light blue, devouring crops, eating away at the stables.

But worst of all, it touched my beloved maze. Oh, how my heart hurts to write that! No other tragedy has been able to harm her, it has stood, neat and pristine for almost eight hundred years. The first two rows of hedges are gone now, nothing but smoking twigs and blackened earth. Of course I raced over there.

It was horrible, the girls in white now nothing but wisps, their once luminous faces pale and faded. The maze's voice (if one can call it that) was stilted, confused even. Fragmented. We wept for her, Sabina and I. But she didn't not respond. My leg has become stiff and painful once more, though this is not my highest concern right now. I must figure out how this happened.

February 28th, 1848

I know now why. It was not an accident. Some girl, some stupid little girl has come forward. She claims she saw a ghost, or a demon perhaps. Bright, red eyes and shadows for skin. She claims it was haunting her, mocking her, hurting her. Claims it crawled inside her dreams and made her do things.

But she was not entirely ordinary. Her mother had some seer's blood in her apparently, the kind that pulls tarot cards and reads your fortune. Perhaps she had some of this special gift, or perhaps she simply heard the old wives' tales as a girl.

However she got there, she knew what to do.

As I have since found out, copper can make a flame turn blue, and it is through this 'holy and cleansing flame', so unlike the flames of hell, that God works (apparently). Not only that, but she said a Hail Mary as she worked, imbuing the flame with even more of her 'holy power.'

She has been punished, obviously. Severino had a fit, he was angrier than I have ever seen him before. Claimed the fire put his 'poor sister' in danger, but the whole family knows why he is really upset – we share his grief, his pain for the maze. He insisted she was expelled from the convent. The Mother Superior didn't need much persuading it seemed, she never seemed to like the girls in her care at the best of times. A fire starting, demon seeing troublemaker with seer's blood was hardly likely to win her mercy. So at least we have that. The girl has nowhere to go, of course, the convent being her last and only hope. And when the maze is healed, she can extract her revenge. I cling to that hope, a cold comfort but comfort nonetheless. The garden will come to full strength again, will bloom with chaos and power once more. She will punish the girl, and she will even enjoy it. I promise you that. I will protect her, at all costs.

Chapter Eighteen

So Greta knew what was coming: fire.

The whole house burning down to the ground, with her smoldering inside. The irony didn't escape her – she would burn like a witch, convicted just as easily, just as brutally. Well, if that's what they wanted, they were going to have to fight for it, she decided, squaring her shoulders.

She was ready, she felt. She had buckets of water out, the bathtubs full, the bedspreads damp- in fact anything fabric she had doused in water, hoping to forestall as much damage as she could. She even went to the beach, gathering buckets of sand. She was ready.

What did surprise her was that Nicco didn't come alone. A woman was with him, a woman she vaguely recognized as Antonio's mother; the boy who was trapped in her mirror. She had made a few TV appearances after he vanished, asking for information on his whereabouts. Greta had genuine pity for this woman, had often wondered what the right thing to do was. She had flirted with the idea of anonymously gifting the mirror to her as some sort of consolation prize. But it was far too late for that now.

Behind her was Mary-Beth's niece, the one she had briefly met at the hospital. She looked worn and tired, her eyes darting around nervously. Greta wondered if there were others, hanging back, lurking in the darkness. Wanting to be involved, but not quite brave enough to meet the witch on her own doorstep. The whole village must have heard what was going on by now.

Nicco wasn't being very subtle about it. He held torches in his hands, ones that were supposed to decorate beach parties or summer weddings, clearly picked up at the local supermarket. The women held gasoline and copper wiring. The torch light flickered on their faces, illuminating their tired eyes and pursed lips.

"We've got to go in," he whispered to them. "Who knows what else is happening inside there?"

The women were clearly not entirely convinced and exchanged a look of terror. But they squared their shoulders, Antonio's mother in particular. She would do anything for the boy she loved. Greta wanted to warn her, to say...something. But there was nothing she could say. They rapped on the door, clearly a mere formality because a moment later, they slammed a brick through the glass, shattering it. Nicco reached a hand inside and unlocked it from within, pushing the door open with an ominous creek. She had grown to love that sound. It was a warning, as if the very house itself were speaking to her. It was proof of how old this place was, how much it had endured. Pride shot through her. She couldn't let that end here, tonight.

A part of her did feel guilty. A small part of her. It was night now, the full moon beating down in all her glory, the house alive with silver light and scurrying shadows. She knew what was waiting for them all inside, knew the horrors they were about to face. But she hadn't asked them to come, had not invited them in. If they had only just listened to her, she could have helped. She knew that, knew it in her blood. Knew that things would be better, if only they listened. The fact that they hadn't was not a reflection on her.

"I'm going to look for Antonio." She heard one voice whisper, the sound echoing through the house.

"Put down the copper writing while you're at it." Nicco hissed back, "We need as much of it as we can, everywhere. Let's burn this fucker to the ground, the right way."

And with that, she knew she would have no regrets.

She crept out of her room, feet silent on the wooden floors. But she didn't get there first. Nicco's scream made her heart smile, her trust in the house clearly well placed.

He sprinted out of the dining room, pelting up the hallways, desperate to get to the front entrance. *Of course,* she thought snidely, *of course he would be the first to run.*

Calmly, she flicked the lock, leaving him wrenching at a door she knew would not open. Next, the glass, the remnants of the poor window he had shattered not moments before. She bought this down upon him, slashing at his face, his neck, his hands. It wasn't quite as dramatic as she hoped, no blood spurting everywhere. But it clearly hurt, Nicco protecting his eyes, letting out another long scream

"Help! Help! The fire, light it! Light it now!" He called out.

She didn't know where the women were, and at that moment she didn't care.

The eyes had followed him out of the dining room almost lazily, sedately, like a lady being escorted to her chair. For one wild, crazed moment, it reminded Greta of herself. Of the time she had taken Frederick to a beautiful restaurant in Budapest, her heels so high all he had to hold her up, her gait so slow it was almost regal. For just a moment, the image flashed before her eyes, so real she could taste it. Her heart sang with joy, thinking this must be another gift from the house.

But smoke brought her back to the moment. She followed it, trusting the eyes to take care of Nicco. She cursed under her breath, flying up the stairs faster than she knew she was capable of. It was Mary-Beth's niece, desperately trying to start a fire in the middle of her bed. The sheets didn't seem to want to light, curling up in puffs of black smoke rather than the blaze of glory she so clearly wanted. Greta felt so smart then, so proud and self-righteous. They had wanted to hurt her, had wanted to destroy her, just as she suspected.

But the curtains were easier. Those took almost instantly. They burned with such a raging heat, Greta was amazed anyone could stand being in the same room with it at all. And worst of all – the fire was blue. They must have rigged the copper up somehow. Yes, she could just see it wrapped around the curtain rail and down the fabric. And it was spreading quickly, in just a few seconds, the flame leaped from the bottom of the curtains to the top, the roar of fire deafening.

The woman was muttering, under her breath, over and over, "Hail Mary, full of grace, hail Mary, full of grace, hail Mary...'

In that moment, she hated them more than ever. Hated that they wanted to destroy her, when they did not even know her. Rage poured out of her. As soon as she thought of doing something, she did it, seeming to have no filter between impulsive emotion and actual action.

The woman just had time to look up, face contorted with horror and shock, before Greta threw her back into the flaming curtains. Her clothes went up instantly, the room soon filled with the scent of burning flesh. But it was her own stupidity that spelt her end. In her shock and pain, she reared back, falling through the window and landing with a crash. Greta peered out after her, pleased to see that she wasn't actually dead, but impaled on the fence, chest forced up unnaturally, blood pooling around her. Good. The house preferred live flesh, and she would hate to take that away from it.

Now it was only the mother left to deal with. But the flames had spread. She must have been the most successful, because the whole first floor seemed to be burning, no longer distinct rooms, but simply a sea of blue flame. The paint popped and ran, the frescos she had once admired now long gone, nothing but streaks of red and black on yellow walls. Greta's heart ached for it. Such beauty, all gone. Everything had ever loved, ripped from her. She couldn't just stand by and let it happen.

Fortunately, the last survivor was easy to find, her calls of "Hail Mary" screamed above the din. Greta could tell it hurt the house. The eyes seemed to be incapable of drawing near, squinting in something that might be considered pain.

She didn't hesitate. She pulled the woman's head back by her hair, forcing her to look into the mirror. To see her son. Her face twisted with pain and shock – maybe even happiness, looking at him as if he were a saint.

"Antonio," she breathed, tears streaming down her face. Somehow, Greta knew they were tears of joy.

"If you die here," she said, her voice strong and powerful, "you can stay with him. In there, in the mirror, forever. Or you can leave. I'll let you go. Which will it be?"

The woman didn't hesitate.

"Antonio. My boy, my angel, my son. I want to be with him," she said. And Greta understood, so well and so completely. In an ocean of chaos and fire, she felt a kind of peace wash over her, knowing exactly what to do. She snapped the woman's neck.

With the Hail Mary finally silenced, the eyes took over. The pipes burst, spraying water everywhere, filing the house with steam. The buckets she had so carefully laid out cascaded over, how she didn't know, she didn't need to know. It was brutal, brutally hot and brutally destructive. But it worked.

The fires cooled, the flames went out. And once more, there was blessed silence. Greta drifted through the charred remains of her house, picking up the little things that mattered. The jewelry Frederick had given her. The perfume bottles Violet had loved. And of course, Floppy. Wet, charred and smoky, she was only barely recognizable as an owl any more, one wing half burnt away.

So the two of them sat together, on the bitter remains of what she had once loved. But looking around, she was proud. Not of hurting people, of course not. But of defending herself, of doing what they said could not be done. Of being so vibrant, reckless and wild – that she had changed everything.

As she gathered her little things, her trinkets that most would think useless, she smiled, humming a tune. Now that she could look around properly, she realized the house was not completely destroyed. It was really only the first level, and even that seemed structurally sound. The second was damaged to be sure, but still standing. The third seemed miraculously untouched.

They had won.

Eventually, the police came. Greta has not bothered to call them, feeling certain that someone else would. A house in flames did not go easily unnoticed. She wasn't disappointed. They swarmed the house, eventually putting out any smoldering cinders that still lingered. News spread fast of course, yet more deaths at that horrible house. Greta wasn't bothered though. People should listen to the rumors, they should stay away. That's what she wanted, and she really didn't understand why people were not taking the hint.

STRANGE AND TWISTED THINGS

Perhaps they would now, she fantasized. Perhaps they would leave her in peace. It was too much to think that they might actually respect her, pity or horror seemed to be the only fate for a woman like her.

But what gave her the most joy, what made her want to sing out with pleasure, was the diary. Her half was still in her pocket, unharmed. The middle pages she collected easily from across the floor, marveling that they too were unburned.

"It's a miracle," she whispered. "Thank you, thank you!"

All that was left now was the ending, the part that Nicco had. Considering that he was now trapped inside the house, forever, she wasn't much worried. She could always hunt him down.

May 14th, 1848

Well. It is done. Or at least, the right seeds have been sown. After the multiple fires and various tragedies at the convent, our family generously stepped in. The sisters could not financially recover after losing half their land to that stupid girl and her 'ghosts', and were forced to move elsewhere. We bought it all. I had the convent ripped down, brick by brick, and every day I smiled more. I built the most wonderful house instead, my home. My real home, designed by me. It takes after the English style, of course. Like my childhood home, but better. No courtyard to speak of, though we will have frescos on the walls, illuminated by grand windows and decadent chandeliers.

And best of all...I got my door. The one I dreamed of while locked away in that wretched, filthy place. It is bright red, just as I hoped, with the exact carving I designed. It is mine, everything behind it is mine, and that will never change.

Best of all, we are so close to the maze! I can visit every day, and I do. It heals, slowly. I dare say it will take many years for it to fully grow back, but with time and care, I have no doubt it will be as luscious as ever. I think it is proud of me.

We had the most wonderful party, the first night our new home was fit for guests. Severino wore black and green, his silent way to honor the maze, and the nighttime. We danced the whole evening through, a string quartet accompanying us. I do not think I have ever been so happy. To add an extra layer of joy...I do believe I am pregnant! We certainly celebrated enough that night. I thank the maze every day for its bounty.

I have decided to hide my diary, lock it away in the basement. Perhaps someone will see it one day, perhaps fate will open the door – my door – to someone worthy. I would never let anyone else enter.

I will try and visit you occasionally, but, to be honest, I am not very good at keeping my word.

July 5th, 1858

This time of year always makes me think of you, and yet I have not written in some time. I have just been so very busy. My three children, Adolpho, Rosa and Annabella, keep me quite occupied. I am proud to say that I am a far more involved mother than my own was, although that hurts in some ways. I cannot imagine abandoning them the way she did with me. I would not even consider turning my back on them, deal with the devil or no. I call them my little demons, a kind of joke between my husband and I. But in truth I see no ill effects on them, apart from the fact that my daughters are total terrors, who will never accept any husband apart from one of their choosing, and my son will defend them to the hilt. Aberrant indeed. I am so very proud of them.

I just wanted to let you know I'm alright. Severino continues to be the perfect husband – frankly I am shocked we do not have even more children. (Although I believe another is on the way!)

The maze flourishes. We continue to send leaves to my in-laws, we have quite the little business going, people want them so badly! I do not know why, and I do not care to know.

I am not ashamed of myself. As I watch my family grow, as I enjoy every day, knowing it is a gift given to me – divine or otherwise. I care only that it is a gift, it is mine, and I have earned it. I am ready to pay the price, whenever that may be. I am not afraid.

Epilogue

It would take a great deal of work to get the house back to a liveable standard, Greta knew that. But she wasn't afraid of a little hard work, and she now had confidence in herself, confidence that she could handle all manner of strange things.

Still, she was surprised when she started to have visitors. A family, well, a pregnant woman and her young child. The father had died recently, it seemed. Or simply abandoned them, the mother didn't like to speak about it.

Greta watched them walk through the rooms, so damaged by fire and water it seemed as if she had never been there at all, all her good work gone to waste. Still, the mother (she would soon learn her name was Andrea) was completely enamored by what was left – the spiral staircase, the tall windows, the cherry floors. She could see that it was beautiful, beautiful beyond all the soot and sadness.

Greta liked that.

They would come and go, measuring things and talking excitedly about their plans. Greta usually waited for them in the living room, by far her favorite place in the house now, she could spend hours there, humming tunes that reminded her of Frederick, or recalling how soft Delta had been, stretched out by her side. She was glad he hadn't been with her during the fire. That would have been a tragedy.

Still, as night fell, she was surprised to find herself in her wedding dress again. She hadn't planned on doing anything special that night, had not scared the villagers in quite some time in fact. But it also felt normal, natural even. Why not wear it? It was expensive, no need for it to go to waste. Besides, even wearing it felt like a celebration of her love for Fredrick, and she would never shy away from that. That love gave her power. It was love for him, of course it was, for every strange habit he had, for every flaw and every perfection.

But it was love *by* her, created, sustained and maintained, by her, built into a work of art. A love story worthy of generations. She made that, not him.

She was rather more surprised when finally, after so many nights of simply watching, of never dreaming of being anything more than an audience member, it happened. Violet finally reached out her hand to Greta.

Shocked, Greta did nothing. But the young woman smiled, nodding her head as if to say 'it's alright'. Shaking just slightly, Greta accepted. She was pulled up and out of her chair, and into that joyous dance. She had seen it so many times, she knew exactly what to do, though she couldn't imagine she was half as handsome as Severino. And then she caught sight of herself in the mirror.

She gasped, beaming at what she saw. She was young, and beautiful again. All signs of The Ugliness now gone, her skin was clear and radiant, her hair dark and full, not a gray wisp to be seen. She gripped Violet's hand under hers, shocked to find it solid and real. She was so happy.

"Mum!" the child wailed, his voice filling the whole house and then some, leaking out into the garden. "This is creepy! I don't like it here!" It was morning now, the child just waking up in time for school, the last of the winter night falling down.

"What is it now?" Andrea asked, lumbering her way into his room. She was clearly very far along in her pregnancy, each step stiff and painful.

"This thing," he said, pointing at an old, stuffed owl.

"Oh," Andrea said, picking the toy up and inspecting it. Its once white fur was now gray and patchy, signs of a hard life. "Yes, I suppose it is rather. I'll get rid of it." So she did, throwing it in the bin when she'd dropped him off at school.

"No," Greta said, to no one in particular. "I think you're going to stay right here." With that, Floppy reappeared, exactly where he had been. So it would happen every time, every time he was hurt, damaged or even touched, he would reappear again. Next to the child's bed, in the mother's desk, wherever really. It didn't matter to Greta, in fact she liked finding new places for him. Liked feeling that flash of horror whenever he was found again. It made her feel powerful, as if she truly had the respect she deserved. After all, the whole house was Floppy's, no matter what the family did. He had come first. She had come first, and she refused to be forgotten.

Finally, finally Greta was able to accept it. She had never created a will, and so, her guess was that the house, upon her death (whenever that was) had gone to her brother. As he was missing, it went to his son, who was also nowhere to be found, and so in the end, it must have gone to his wife.

Greta looked her over, the woman's face round and adorned with nothing but cheerful looking glasses. She hoped Andrea was better than her husband, stronger than her father-in-law. That would remain to be seen. She could feel Andrea's brittle hope, her fledgling plans for a new life.

STRANGE AND TWISTED THINGS 217

"This is my house. And I welcome you as a guest," Greta said, and in the shrill darkness of the night, she felt that maybe the mother could hear her.

"But you will play by my rules."

Andrea shivered, pulling the sheets closer. She could have sworn she had heard something, some deep, dark creaking in the house. A whispered secret trailing down the hall. But of course, it was old, and badly damaged, barely liveable. Naturally there would be sounds. She pushed the fear deeper down inside her, determined not to give in. She was now totally alone in the world, with a child to care for and one more on the way. Even the neighbors here seemed distinctly unfriendly, none had come to visit her, most seemed to actively avoid the house. There was no one to turn to and nowhere to run.

No, she decided, screwing her eyes shut tightly. *The house can't be cursed, because curses are not real,* she told herself yet again. There was a logical reason for everything, there had to be. There certainly wasn't an unnatural chill in the air, or a basement door that refused to be opened, that had somehow avoided the fire damage. And she would never admit just how frightening she found the old woman's room, with the smashed window that had taken far too long to repair, the glass and wood resisting her as if it didn't want to be fixed, didn't want to be glossed over.

For just one moment, she let her mind wander down the stairs, across the garden and to the mailbox. It was so stiff and heavy, she had to yank it open, the rusted metal screaming each time. And yet every day, it drifted open at exactly 2:00, swaying slightly, as if someone were madly searching for something. Sometimes she watched it from the window, just to be sure she wasn't going mad, that no one was playing pranks on her.

And in the deep dark of the night, she lost herself in knots of worry and fear, the old tales of ghosts and demons coming back to her in waves.

"No," she muttered into her pillow, "none of that is real."

It was nothing.

Acknowledgements

The first draft of this book was written in eight days. It was a wild and tumultuous time, and this manuscript was very much born out of that. Although I'd had the basic idea for some time, the actual plotting, outlining and writing all occurred within a very particular time of my life. I doubt I could write it again now. But it couldn't become the polished piece it is today without the help of my mother, who must have read it a dozen times, offering invaluable feedback and countless tips along the way. And of course to my Aunt Kristen who has been a massive help with this book, and all my others! Also, a huge thanks for my editor, Sarah De Souza, who saw this book to the finish line and cheered the whole way. The editing process was much more laborious than the actual writing, as is often the case. It was examined by multiple Beta readers, all of whom I owe a read in return.

Of course none of this would have been at all possible without my wife, Iris, whose unending support I will never be able to repay. Thank you, my darling for being everything you are. And then of course, to my muse, Matt. This book certainly would not have been written without you, make of that what you will! Also, to my cats who, by and large, were kind enough to stay off the key board.

Also by Holly Payne-Strange

All Of Us Alone

They survived the destruction of their planet- now the real test begins on ours.

In the dead of night, an alien family crashes into the middle of New Mexico. Refugees from across the stars, they've only just escaped a planet wide catastrophe when they arrive on Earth. But they are not given a warm welcome.

The remnants of their crashed spacecraft are swiftly appropriated by the US military, stranding them entirely. Adapting to this unwelcoming new world becomes their only choice, and a single misstep could mean death- or worse, brutal experimentation. As they grapple with the strange terrain of Earth, they must choose between their true selves and survival, deciding what to relinquish for a chance at life. What must they give up in order to thrive on earth? And what's more, how could they even know?

Coming December 2023

Printed in Great Britain
by Amazon